SILVER & GOLD

SILVER IN THE CITY

A.D. ELLIS

1

BENJAMIN "BENJI" SILVER

MY PHONE RANG. Saved by the bell. I was *not* looking forward to more questions about my overnight guest, Rhys. It had been shit luck that we overslept and he had to dart past my roommates that morning. Rhys was amazing in bed and we got along well, but we were both committed to setting up our new art businesses. I had the feeling that trying to combine our artistic talents and endeavors in anything more serious than sex would bring on a whole host of issues. So, we hooked up and didn't bring our art or business into the mix. Clearly the relationship wasn't going anywhere and would likely fizzle once we both got our studios up and running.

However, my twin brother, Bode, his boyfriend, Sage, and my cousin, Kyson would have *loved* to keep peppering me with questions about Rhys.

And if you're being honest, the relationship could be going somewhere and you'd be okay with it. I really liked the guy—more so than any guy I'd ever hooked up with or dated—

but we both had other things going on. Best to keep it casual.

But more than casual would be so good.

I ignored that niggling thought. "Hello?" I paused and listened, making eye contact with my roomies.

"Benji, it's Kris," my realtor spoke on the other end of the phone. "Are you available to meet?" Kris was a great realtor and never beat around the bush. I liked her directness.

"Yes." I nodded as I spoke before allowing Kris to continue.

"Would you be able to meet me at the new building in a couple hours?"

"Yeah, that will work fine." I was so excited to get my new building, I was willing to run down the damn street if she needed me to. I was chomping at the bit to open my art studio and shop.

"Great, hoping to get final paperwork signed." Kris rustled some papers.

"Looking forward to it."

"Ok, be careful. See you then." Another phone rang on Kris' side.

"Yeah, you too. Thanks. See you then." I had to fight the grin attempting to overtake my face.

When I hung up, I couldn't help the huge grin I turned toward the guys. "That was my realtor. Says I should come down to the new building today and sign some final paperwork."

They all whooped and slapped me on the back.

"About fucking time." Bode pulled me in for a hug.

I sighed and ran a hand over my face. "I've been waiting so long to have a studio and place of my own. I'm tired of renting shared studio space. I want to be able to create, teach, and sell all in one location. *The Silver Creative* is one step closer to reality."

Two hours later, the four of us trooped down the stairs of our shared apartment and walked a few blocks to where my new building was located. It was an older space, but it had been completely renovated and both the exterior and interior were spectacular.

We entered the building and were greeted by my realtor, Kris. She frowned.

"What's up? Something fall through?" My face adopted the same serious expression as my heart fell to my knees.

"Well, it appears there's been a bit of a snafu the likes of which I've never dealt with." Kris continued to frown.

I crossed my arms over my chest and scowled just as the door opened and two people walked in.

A flash of dark blond hair, dark-rimmed glasses, and a tall, strong build caught my eye.

Rhys? Why would a guy I'd had a few casual hookups with be at my closing? "What are you doing here?" I demanded even as my heart flipped-flopped.

"Could ask you the same thing." Rhys stopped and looked at his own realtor with a questioning scowl.

Another person entered the front door. An older man who looked nervous like he thought we might hurt him.

"Ah, yes. Well, I see we're all present and accounted for." The man wrung his hands. "I must say, this is not something I have experience with, but I'm sure we can get it all worked out. Just some miscommunication, I'm sure." I halfway expected him to pull a silk hanky from his pocket and dab at his brow.

"What's the problem?" Rhys asked.

"Well, it appears that both a Mr. Rhys Golden *and* a Mr. Benjamin Silver have leased this building through what I'm assuming is a paperwork mix-up." The older man grimaced. "An interesting and unfortunate predicament, but one I'm most sure we can set to right."

Around the room, mouths dropped open and eyes widened.

I frowned.

Rhys frowned.

Bode whistled.

"What the actual fuck," I murmured under my breath and took a deep breath. This couldn't be happening. I'd been working to get this building leased for months and had a lot of money sunk into setting up my studio.

"No way, I want this building. It's perfect for my studio. I'm not sharing it with him." Rhys crossed his arms over his chest and jutted his chin.

"Well, I'm not sharing with you either, so maybe you should find your own spot," I spat back. As much as Rhys and I got along in the bedroom, I'd known I was right in predicting we would totally clash in our art businesses.

"Gentlemen, gentlemen, please. Let's gather at the table and discuss particulars." The older gentleman turned pleading eyes our way.

"You want us to stay?" Bode asked.

I pinched the bridge of my nose. I wanted them there, but I didn't expect them to give up their time to sit through what I was guessing was going to be a shit show. "You don't have to."

Bode nodded. "We'll stay."

My heart warmed as Bode, Sage, and Kyson fell into

step beside me as I followed Kris to the table near the back. Maybe I imagined it, but Rhys appeared irritated that I had my brother and friends as backup.

Once the entire group was seated, the gentleman began. "I'm Mr. Scott. I'm the liaison between the lessor of the building, Mr. Franklin, and the lessees, Mr. Golden and Mr. Silver."

"This building was not open for joint lease nor does my client wish to enter into a joint lease." Kris rested her elbows on the table and spoke firmly.

"I'm highly concerned as to how a mistake like this could even happen," Rhys's realtor chimed in. She seemed slightly less blunt than Kris, but I could tell she was ready to fight.

"I'm sorry, we didn't meet." I directed my comment toward her in an attempt to stay civil. "I'm Benji Silver."

She smiled kindly despite the frustration filling the room. "I'm Kristy Smith. Mr. Golden's realtor."

All of a sudden, the mysterious mistake began to make sense.

Paperwork with realtor names of Kris Smith and Kristy Smith, lessee names of Silver and Golden, an aging man who maybe wasn't as sharp as he once was. Didn't make the screw-up any less of a huge frustration, but at least it kinda made more sense as to how it happened.

Mr. Scott scrunched up his face and fumbled with paperwork in a folder. "Ah, yes. It appears that perhaps some name mix-ups are at the heart of this situation. I do, by all means, accept responsibility for my part in the mistake." He sorted papers into two stacks. "Kris Smith with client Benjamin Silver. Kristy Smith with client Rhys Golden. I do believe I've been duped by similar names."

Kris breathed deeply.

Kristy sighed and leaned back in her chair.

Rhys rolled his eyes.

I frowned, but I felt a little sorry for the old man.

Two hours later, after hashing and rehashing the errors and options, Rhys and I stared daggers at each other over the table.

"This situation is annoying. Despite the name mix-ups, numbers and such should have been paid attention to and set the files apart." Kris made a few final scribbles on a legal pad. "However, the time and cost to repair the damage done would tie up both Mr. Silver's and Mr. Golden's time and money. It is my professional opinion," she glanced between Rhys and me, "that Benji and Rhys should jointly lease the building."

"But we both paid the full down payment," Rhys cut in.

"Both down payments will be applied toward the monthly lease payments," Mr. Scott cut in as if pleading for us to save him the legalities of fixing this monumental screw-up.

Rhys and Kristy conversed quietly for a moment.

Kris leaned over to me. "Honestly, this is a huge fuck up and I have *no* clue how it got to the point of closing without being caught—never should have happened—but if you two can agree to share the space for at least the year, you'll save attorney fees and the loss of a huge chunk of time."

I took a deep breath and glanced at Bode. He pressed his lips together and shrugged sympathetically.

"I'd like to discuss some particulars with Kris, but I

think we can work this out. *If* the guys are willing to share." Kristy glanced between Rhys and me.

"What kind of particulars?" I asked and didn't miss that Mr. Scott seemed relieved I'd asked the question.

"Extra time on the lease for the same previously agreed upon monthly payments." The look on Kristy's face dared Mr. Scott to argue.

"So, we'd basically be paying the same amount of money divided by a longer lease, so lower monthly payments?" I repeated what I thought she was saying.

"Exactly. I'm sure Mr. Scott and Mr. Franklin will agree this *fix* is much easier than dragging attorneys into the mix." Kristy raised her brows.

Mr. Scott nodded. "Yes, yes. I'm sure our attorney can draw up paperwork relating to the longer lease and make sure everything is legit."

"Too bad it couldn't have been legit the first time." Rhys's brows were drawn together. He was the poster child for hipster. Gorgeous, rugged yet well-groomed, dressed in fashion boots, jeans, a button-up, thin tie, and leather jacket. He made me drool. But he also pissed me off.

After a few more comments and clarifications, the group dispersed.

Rhys and Kristy met with Kris and myself outside of the building.

"I'll be in touch. We'll get all of this straightened out and you two can probably take possession within a week." Kristy shook my hand and then Kris's. "This is definitely a first for me and I'll be damned if I know how the hell it made it this far, but you guys are getting a great building at an amazing price. I know it's not ideal, but I'm sure you can make your artistic differences work."

Kris nodded in agreement although she looked frustrated on my behalf.

"I guess we don't really have a choice," Rhys bit out angrily.

"Well, you do. But I'm not sure your choices are any better than this option." Kris wrinkled her nose.

"We'll meet up and work through plans for setting up." I gave a nod to Rhys.

"You two should probably exchange numbers," Kristy suggested.

My cheeks heated and Rhys coughed.

"He's got my number," I mumbled.

"Wait, you two know each other?" Kristy clapped her hands together. "Well, that should make this sharing a building thing a whole lot easier, right?"

I pressed my lips together in a fake smile. "Right."

Rhys raised his brows. "Sure."

* * *

"Man, I'm really sorry for the shit show this turned out to be." Bode slapped me on the back before pouring shots for everyone as we sat around The Salty Lizard.

Sage wrinkled his nose. "I'm guessing Mr. Scott is at the heart of the mix-up and maybe should be thinking of retiring. Or at least not dealing with the paperwork part of the job."

Kyson stood behind me and rubbed my shoulders. "Come in tomorrow, you can be one of my first real customers. I'll give you the royal treatment. The knots in your muscles have their own knots."

Kyson's new place, *Mass. Ave. Massage Therapy*, was doing a slow opening this week. Open House, samples, drawings for prizes, and all that jazz. He was looking to build his client list and planned to do that by offering some incentives to get people into the office. Kyson was as laid back as ever and knew it would take a while to grow his customer base. I'd had his massages, they were amazing. I planned on advertising for him at *The Silver Creative*.

Shit.

Two thoughts hit me at once.

Today was the Open House at *Mass. Ave. Massage*.

And my business name of *The Silver Creative* wasn't likely to go over well with Rhys.

Fucking shit.

The four of us took our shots and chatted a bit about how crumby my situation was. But I was tired of the topic, so I switched to something happier.

"Look, Rhys and I will get this worked out. We may kill each other in the process, but we should change the subject." I stacked the glasses.

"Rhys is the same guy who snuck out of your room this morning, right?" Bode mused as he rolled the bottom of his shot glass on the bar.

"Yeah," I hedged. I'd never been one to tell all about my hookups, but Bode would press.

"So, the sex is good, but working together may kill you?" My twin narrowed his eyes.

"No." I sighed. "The sex is amazing. Or *was*. But we clash in our artistic endeavors. Our ideas don't mesh. Our plans and goals are very different." I ran a hand over my face. "Or maybe it's more accurate to say that our plans and goals and ideas are very similar and that's the problem? Fuck, I don't even know."

"Well, this should be *very* interesting." Kyson finished rubbing my shoulders and neck.

"Let's talk about the Open House." I threw out a life preserver in hopes of saving myself. "Starts at two o'clock, right?"

Kyson's eyes sparkled. "Yep. You guys still willing and able to come help?"

We all agreed and trooped upstairs to the apartment to get ready.

The rest of the day was spent assisting Kyson spread the word and hopefully pull in some loyal new clients.

I'd deal with the Rhys and studio situation later.

2

RHYS GOLDEN

I STUCK my head through the backdoor at my older sister's house on the far north side of Indianapolis the day before Benji and I were set to move into the building. Caroline's late husband had left her and the children with enough money that she didn't have to work. My sister kept busy with volunteering and charity work. Her children, my niece and nephew, were grown and on their own, but younger than me.

"You home?" I asked as I walked into the kitchen and angrily snatched an apple from the designer fruit bowl.

"Oh, grumpy and gloomy." Caroline breezed into the room and gave me a hug. "I suppose drama follows these moods?" She gestured toward the coffee pot with a raised brow.

I shook my head. "Can we do tea?" I finished my apple in about four chomps and slumped into a chair at the table. I'd come over to work in my cramped studio space Caroline allowed me to keep in her basement, but I decided I needed to vent before I could create.

As she prepared two mugs of tea, Caroline eyed me. "Tell me what ails you."

I held my face in both hands and groaned.

"That bad?" Caroline stirred the mugs of tea and brought them to the table. "Boy troubles? Business troubles? Creativity troubles?"

"Yes," I grumbled and breathed deeply behind my hands.

"Oh, dear. A trifecta." She picked up both mugs and headed out of the kitchen. "Come on, this sounds more serious than a kitchen table chat."

I followed her to her den. The area was one of the most peaceful and comfortable places I'd ever seen. Soft, cushy seating, wispy window coverings, calming light, and diffused essential oils immediately brought a sigh of relief to my lips. We sat and got comfortable. We sipped our tea. Caroline waited.

Caroline was twelve when I was born. She'd been my first best friend, my first babysitter, my first confidant. My sister knew I tended toward moody, self-absorbed, and occasionally dramatic.

I knew these things about myself as well. Sometimes those characteristics were things I strived to improve upon, sometimes they were just part of the real me. That particular day, my moody, dramatic, self-absorbed ass wanted to gripe, complain, wallow, and have my sister show me the proper amount of pity.

"So, I've been seeing a guy." My heart fluttered at even the slightest thought of Benji. *Ugh.* I did *not* need my heart fluttering over a casual hookup.

Caroline nodded as she sipped her tea and watched me.

"The sex is amazing. And we were really starting to have a connection outside of the bedroom." My stomach clenched. Maybe I was the only one who had thought we were connecting on more than a sexual level.

"But?"

"Well, that involves my second problem." I took several moments to explain the snafu with the lease. "So now, thanks to some name mix-ups and an aging man who should probably retire, we're forced to share a building." I sighed. Overdramatic, yes, but it was my pity party and I'd be dramatic if I wanted to. "Obviously, our relationship is over."

Caroline frowned. "Why would a fledgling relationship that was possibly beginning to be more than just sex have to be over?"

"Benji is an artist." I waved a hand dismissively.

She raised a brow and waited.

"We work in some similar mediums, but our pieces are almost as different as you can get." I took a drink of my tea and savored the rich flavor. I worked in mostly assemblage art, and metal and wood sculpture. I dabbled in painting here and there. Benji worked with clay and various ceramics to create vases, cups, pots, decorative pieces, and jewelry. He also painted abstract art and landscapes.

"And you can only be with another artist if they make the exact same art as you?" Caroline posed the question innocently, but I knew she was digging in to make a point.

"No, but this building was to be *my* studio, *my* place to sell my work. Now I have to split the studio space, compete for customers, hope I sell as well as Benji." My brows drew together as I took another drink of tea.

"Ah, yes. Quite a dilemma." Caroline nodded, slightly raised one brow, and hid a smile behind her tea cup.

My anger flared as my sister humored me. She clearly thought I was being ridiculous. She just wasn't getting it.

"Benji is so much like me in a lot of ways. We're passionate, creative, driven. He's as determined, competitive, and stubborn as I am." I shook my head. "Some of those similarities are great, some aren't so great. But we're very different too. He dresses in sleek, casual style. Lots of black. I'm like the quintessential hipster." I didn't know why it seemed important to point out how similar and different we were, as if it would explain why I was worked into such a tizz.

Caroline finished her tea. "So, you like this guy. The sex is great. You've got things in common, yet plenty of differences as well."

I nodded, feeling glum.

"And it won't work, why?" My sister crunched her face.

"Great sex and similarities aren't the most solid base for a business relationship we're being forced into." Seriously, how was she not seeing this?

"Maybe give yourselves some time to settle in at the new business setup? Then revisit the relationship?"

"He's going to *teach* art too! How will I compete with that?" I nearly knocked over my cup with a wild gesture.

"Does it have to be a competition?" Caroline trailed her finger in a circular motion on the pillow she held.

I started to snap back, but found myself opening and closing my mouth. "I guess it doesn't *have* to be a competition, but I don't really see how it won't be."

"If you let it." Caroline raised a brow.

"You've known me my whole life. When have I ever

been laid back and not been competitive over my work?" I didn't even try to stop the eye roll. We were talking about *me*. I wasn't the easiest person to get along with.

"Valid point." She pulled a blanket over her lap. "But I also know you've never really talked about a great sexual partner and possible connected relationship before. You're usually booting them out at the exact moment a slight imperfection is noticed."

I sighed. "Yeah, up until this building screwup, I was thinking Benji may have been a possible candidate for a real relationship." I hugged a pillow to my chest. "I was really letting myself get my hopes up." My heart squeezed as I whispered the words.

"Nobody, and no relationship, is perfect." Caroline nudged me with her foot.

"I just want what Mom and Dad had." My eyes stung. My parents had passed away when I was a pre-teen, but I still recalled how much in love and happy they were. It's what I wanted, what I dreamed of, what I measured every possible relationship by.

"Rhys Alexander Golden," Caroline scolded good-naturedly, "I've told you time and time again that you've got selective memory about Mom and Dad. You were likely too young to pick up on their imperfections, but I promise they were there. No person is perfect. No relationship is perfect. Don't throw away someone who makes you happy because you're afraid you guys might not be able to work well together."

"That's the other part of the problem. My creativity was going great until the building issue and now my head and heart act as if I've never created a piece of art in my life." I threw my head back against the fluffy couch. "The trifecta of issues bringing me drama and gloom kinda suck."

Caroline was quiet for a bit. "Maybe you're bringing some of the drama and gloom on yourself?"

I clenched my teeth. I was *not* in the mood for a lecture.

"I'm just saying," she held up her hand to fend off my protests, "give it all some time. Work with Benji to get your business set up. Maybe sharing the building will work out better than either of you could even imagine." She bit back a smirk when I scoffed. "Give your art some time to ramp back up. You've always ebbed and flowed through your work." She leaned forward and patted my leg. "And don't push Benji away. You've got a sparkle in your eyes despite the gloom, and I have a feeling he's the one who put that gleam there. Don't count out a relationship with him."

I huffed and rolled my eyes. Sometimes she just didn't get me at all, and she definitely wasn't getting this situation. It was all too much. I needed to focus on my art and the business, I didn't have the energy or time to put effort into a relationship that would never live up to my idea of perfect. I stood. "Thanks for the tea and talk. I'm going to the basement to work. I'll start moving stuff out over the next few days."

For the next two hours, I threw myself into an assemblage piece consisting of gears, pulleys, springs, and rulers. It was a large piece that I hoped to finish soon. I planned to have several large and small pieces along with my metal and wood sculptures displayed and on sale at my new studio.

My new studio?

No.

Fuck.

Our new studio.

Was I being selfish and bratty? Yes. I could admit that. But, damn it, I wanted that building to myself. I had worked hard to open my own studio and sales floor. I didn't want to share.

I sighed and finished the piece. I loaded up three boxes of supplies and small pieces in my car. I'd start moving into the building tomorrow.

As I drove to my apartment, I thought of Benji. Thoughts of his gorgeous body, his quiet humor, his good heart all bombarded me. For a brief moment, I allowed myself to call to mind the way his skin felt under my hand, the heat of his body on mine, the catch in his breathing and the whimpers he made as I fucked him. I squeezed my eyes shut. No, I needed to forget all of that and focus only on my art and the studio.

3

BENJI

I PLANNED to arrive at the building early so I could get the key from Kris and be inside before Rhys. Clearly, great minds think alike because as I walked toward the building, I recognized Rhys's form leaning against the front window.

He was so fucking beautiful it nearly took my breath away.

I was dressed in my usual black, fitted shirt, dark jeans, and a pair of dark fashion sneakers. Nothing special. Rhys would claim he wasn't dressed to impress, and he likely wasn't, but his cuffed dark jeans with a peek of green socks, gray leopard spotted canvas shoes, light gray V-neck t-shirt, and brushed silk floral jacket all paired with dark aviator sunglasses—he'd obviously opted for his contacts instead of the dark-rimmed glasses he sometimes wore—not only looked effortlessly pieced together, but also invited my eyes to drink him in and my heart to pound. So damn gorgeous.

I knew under those jeans were strong, pale legs

carpeted with light strawberry blonde hair. I remembered the width of his chest, the heat of his arms around me, the press of his dick against my ass, and the sting his stubble left on my thighs, my neck, my chin. I wanted to grab his hand and drag him back to my bedroom, fall into bed, open my body for him, and forget all the mess having to do with the building.

But no. I couldn't do that. I'd worked for too hard and too long to get my own business, my own studio, my own space. Being a twin meant that very little was ever *mine*. Bode was my best friend, a part of me I'd never give up—would die if I lost him—but he was also the twin who got more attention. Whether because his big personality demanded it or because his school issues growing up necessitated it. I didn't hold it against him, it just helped to explain my deep desire to have something that was all me. All mine. All Benji.

And now I had to share it with Rhys.

I wanted to share my body with Rhys. Share a dinner. Share a movie date. But I didn't want to share my building.

I needed to work on my phrasing. It wasn't *my* building. It was *our* building. I hated the way it sounded. Things had always been *ours* when I was growing up. I sighed deeply. Fighting with the man and throwing a tantrum wasn't going to change our situation. I put a smile on my face, pushed down my sour feelings over sharing, dismissed the way my skin longed to recall the heat of Rhys's body against mine, and held my hand out.

"Morning. Ready to do this?" I asked with a lot more positivity and friendliness than I was truly feeling. Fake it 'til you make it, I guess.

Rhys glared at me. Well, I assumed he was glaring behind his mirrored sunglasses, but he shook my hand. "Morning. Yeah, let's get started."

I ignored the heat of his touch and the images of his hands all over my body. Kris and Kristy had agreed Kris would drop the keys to us this morning and I recognized her car pulling up at that moment. After a few pleasantries were exchanged, Rhys and I were left standing in front of our new building with our keys. As much as I wanted to do the honors of unlocking and entering *my* place, I pocketed my key and gestured toward the door. It didn't seem as special now that we both had keys.

Rhys pressed his lips together and nodded as he slid the key in the lock and pushed the door open. "I unloaded some boxes at the back door." He slipped his key onto a key ring. "I'm going to get those carried in."

"Yeah, I'll get my first round unloaded as well. Best to use the backdoor I think. Try not to clog up the front sidewalk and don't want unwanted interest just yet. Once everything is inside and we can lock up, we can start making our presence known a bit more." I pulled my phone from my pocket and texted Bode. He'd agreed to deliver my things with his truck before he and Sage had a morning date.

An hour later, Rhys and I stood among a large number of boxes near the backdoor. We both had our hands on our hips and I'm sure the look on Rhys's face mirrored mine in silently saying *where the fuck do we start*?

"Well, let's take a look at the upstairs area first and see how we want to split that up. Then we can figure out the studio space." I waved my arm toward the stairs and followed up behind Rhys. I did my best not to stare at his amazing ass, but it was a losing battle.

"I really like the area up here." Rhys glanced around the upstairs space.

It was well-suited as a living space, although neither of us were planning to live there full-time. The area needed a lot of work if it was going to be sold as a livable space, but it was workable for sure.

"I like that we can keep food in the pantry and fridge, wash dishes, cook. None of the appliances are top-of-the-line, but they are all functional." I turned the knobs on the oven and opened the refrigerator as Rhys turned on the water.

"Yeah. Was thinking of moving a couch and bed up here. Have a place to rest or sleep if needed. Kinda a home away from home?" Rhys crossed his arms over his chest as if daring me to disagree.

I didn't take the bait. It was a good idea. "I've got a couch in storage. You have a bed?"

Rhys nodded. "Bed and a chaise lounge. It's ugly as hell, but it's sturdy and comfortable."

My traitorous mind automatically imagined Rhys bending me over his ugly but sturdy chaise lounge and I coughed to cover it up. I needed to get it through to my head and my dick that what Rhys and I had was over. Had to be.

Right?

I cleared my throat. "There's a bathroom downstairs we can use and keep looking nice for customer use, but this one up here can be more functional for showers and what-not." Just over a week ago, I would have been thinking about using this upstairs space as a little private getaway for Rhys and me. I imagined bringing Rhys to my studio, things getting hot between us as we played out our own little *Ghost* pottery wheel scene, retreating upstairs for a sexy shower and then falling into bed where we fucked each other's brains out all night.

Instead, I shook the vision from my head and sniffed. "We can each grab some soap and shampoo for up here. Keep extras of whatever toiletries we might want or need." I headed toward the stairs. "Let's take a look at the studio space."

The building was set up perfectly for our display floor to span the entire front of the structure with one-third or more of the back being open for our studio space.

We stood at the backdoor and surveyed the area.

"What are your thoughts? I'm thinking our options are one huge studio with a shared storage space and we both have our own little area to work, or divide the space into two halves and each take half. Store our own materials on our own side." I could honestly see pros and cons to both options.

"Well, splitting it in half and having our own sides would offer more privacy. Maybe put up a wall?" Rhys frowned, his arms crossed over his chest.

I narrowed my eyes. "Yeah, I guess I can see that. But we'd lose some space if we went that route." I ran a hand over the back of my neck. "Could set up our main areas at angles where we'd have some privacy. I know I don't like anyone breathing over my shoulder while I work."

"Yeah, keep things private, don't have to worry about originality and stuff."

My eyes grew wide. "You think I'm going to copy your work?" I barked out a humorless laugh. "That's rich." I folded my arms over my chest. "I can assure you that I neither *want* to nor *need* to copy from you. I've seen your work. You've seen mine. We have very different talents and skills and eyes for beauty. Your designs are as safe from me as I would assume my designs are safe from you." I shook my head and scoffed. "You're fucking serious right now, aren't you?"

Rhys's nostrils flared and his jaw clenched. "You saying my work isn't worth your time? I'm so far beneath you that you wouldn't even consider copying me?"

I laughed and bent at the waist to put my hands on my knees. "Holy shitballs, man. You are fucking something else right now, you know that? First, I don't copy. I have my own ideas. Even if you and I were to interpret a theme, we'd both create something completely different. Equally good, but different. Second, you really need to work on your confidence. You're an amazing artist. Period. Believe that."

Rhys fumed quietly for a moment before taking a deep breath. "I'm sorry. I get competitive and I worry my work won't hold its own against yours. Like what if your stuff sells and mine doesn't? Plus, you'll be making money with the lessons you're going to give." He would have given a petulant child a run for their money with his pouting.

"Man, you gotta stop with that shit. You've got a fantastic eye and you make seriously awesome pieces. Your clientele likely won't be the same as mine, but there are plenty of buyers for both of us. I'll likely get more of the casual shoppers who are looking for a decorative piece, a gift, some jewelry, maybe a landscape for their living room." I moved closer to him, feeling shocked that Rhys needed to hear that his work was good enough; the man was beyond talented and I'd never realized he doubted that. "You'll probably get the bigger art collectors, the more serious art connoisseurs, the people looking to drop big bucks on what they consider more professional pieces. A customer buying a vase for their table or a pair of earrings or an ocean scene isn't the same buyer as someone looking for a large-scale sculpture or assemblage piece. The only medium we kinda share is paint, but even then, yours is more large-scale while mine is more wall-hanging size." I understood doubting your work, all creatives did at one time or another, but I was confident and comfortable with my work for the most part. Rhys's doubts about his explained a lot.

My hand brushed against his and my breath hitched. If Rhys moved even slightly, I'd take it as a sign to hold his hand. But he didn't. He stared at me for several moments as if he wanted to say something, wanted to *do* something, but he shook his head and turned away.

"Yeah, so I guess we need to know where you're teaching before we can decide on studio space." He rested his hands on his hips. "Doesn't seem fair you'd get half the studio *and* a teaching area." The sullen child hadn't fully taken his leave just yet.

I gaped. Wow. I'd thought I was self-absorbed, but Rhys was definitely surpassing me right then. "I planned to use that small office/kitchen space for lessons."

"Oh, so we lose an office and kitchen so you can *teach*?"

"Jesus, man. Would you listen to yourself? What are you, thirteen? You're acting like a sniveling brat." I braced both hands behind my head.

Rhys winced. "Sorry. I had big plans for this place and

I'm having to rethink everything now. I'm not purposely being difficult."

Could have fooled me.

"I get it. I had plans too. But I think we can make it work." I gestured toward one side of the room. "The side storage closet is big enough for two desks; it would make a perfect office. As far as the studio is concerned, I feel we'd both have the most room if we make *one* storage area for all of our supplies and section the room by mediums. You'll need your sculpting area and a place for assemblage. We can do one part for painting. I need my wheel and kiln. I'm thinking we order and pay for supplies together. You get the things that only you'll need, I'll get the things that only I'll need, but we go in together on supplies we can share. Do a monthly supply check and order in bulk if we can."

Rhys nodded. "Yeah, we can probably work that out." He glanced at his watch. "Shit, I wanted to get boxes unpacked today before bringing more tomorrow."

"Let's unpack what's here now and break down boxes. Tomorrow we can work on set up of the studio area and the sales floor. Unpack some more. I'd love to be ready for business by next week if possible."

Rhys nodded. We set to work unpacking and breaking down boxes and I turned on some Andrew McMahon music.

"Ugh, we'll need to work on finding a happy medium for music because *that* is not going to cut it," Rhys grumped as he curled his nose and tossed flat cardboard onto the pile.

"What?! You don't like Andrew McMahon? He's great.

I saw him in concert not too long ago." I seriously couldn't believe he didn't like the music.

"He's not exactly my style." Rhys shrugged.

"What's your style? Is there *hipster* music?" I teased with an elbow to his arm.

"I like the Mountain Goats, Me First and the Gimme Gimmes, stuff like that."

I whistled. "Yeah, we'll need to negotiate music. Maybe just a calm Spotify channel of generic music would be best."

Rhys nodded.

It amazed me that Rhys and I were so damn connected and compatible in bed, both super artistically talented, shared a lot of the same personality traits—both positive and negative—and yet we were so very different. Part of me wanted to tackle the challenge of overcoming our differences and allowing the rest to meld together into the relationship I'd *thought* was possibly growing before the building mess up. The other part of me was beyond irritated with his moody, pouty, selfish ass and wanted to think I'd dodged a bullet.

But as I watched him and recalled the fantastic sex and quiet talks in bed, I couldn't help but side with the part of me that wanted to make this work.

Would Rhys even be willing? Did we have the time and energy to put into building a business *and* a relationship? I sighed. Now was not the time to make those decisions. I switched the music to something soft and relaxing just to have some background noise and we worked in comfortable silence for another hour.

I wanted Rhys to pull me into a hug as we finished up and said our goodbyes. Did he want that? I missed his touch, his heat, his strength. I longed for his mouth on mine, his hands cupping my face, his hard body against me. The way Rhys clenched his jaw and clipped out a farewell, he either wanted exactly the same thing, or he couldn't wait to be far away from me.

I trudged home.

Tomorrow would be another day.

* * *

An hour into the next day, I was ready to strangle Rhys.

He likely would have gladly done the same to me.

We were *not* meshing well as we attempted to set up our sales floor.

"I was thinking of putting a sales counter over here and toward the back." I gestured to the area I thought would be perfect for the sales counter.

"Well, I was planning to have a sales counter on the opposite side." Rhys folded his arms.

Of course he was.

"Can figure that out in a bit." I breathed deeply. "With my last name being Silver, I was planning to do mostly brushed silver for most of the fixtures."

Rhys glared. "With my last name being Golden, I was planning most of the fixtures to be a brushed gold."

"I wanted a large area rug. In silver." I pointed to where I'd planned to put a decorative rug.

"I'd been looking at rugs. In gold." Rhys's eyes were hard.

I nodded and fought the urge to cuss and storm off. "Thoughts on a coffee and tea station for the customers as they browse?"

"I planned to have one. And use local bakeries to supply pastries and things." Rhys's cheeks pinked. "Did we just agree on something?"

"Don't get too excited. We haven't discussed color or location just yet." I smiled wryly.

"Maybe we could plan the layout of our displays and then work around that first?" Rhys's words at least *sounded* like he was attempting to cooperate.

"That sounds like our best bet for now."

An hour later, we stood in the middle of our future display store with a scratched-out map and tentative smiles on our faces.

"So, we can't agree on color schemes, décor, and locations of a lot of things, but at least we've got a fairly good idea of where we'd like our pieces displayed." I sighed. We were butting heads on many things; having agreed on the displays was a huge relief.

"I guess we could do separate sales counters and coffee stations and two rugs?" Rhys wrinkled his nose.

I rolled my eyes. "Does that sound like it would be inviting or even close to aesthetically pleasing?"

"No." Rhys ran a hand over his face.

"I want The Silver Creative to be welcoming, a place people feel comfortable, somewhere they want to spend a lot of time and *buy* items." I realized a split second too late the mistake I'd made.

"The *Silver* Creative?" Rhys bit out. He let loose a gravelly, growly sound and huffed away. Five seconds later I heard the backdoor slam.

Fuck.

The Silver Creative was what I'd planned to name my studio from the very first conception of the idea. I understood why Rhys wouldn't be on board, but damn, it hurt to think the name wasn't going to happen.

I glanced around the room and shook my head as I folded up the map. We'd discussed opening next week. As it was, all we had ready were our pieces. We didn't have a name, nothing was set up, we couldn't even agree on a fucking rug. Oh, well we *did* agree we wanted a damn coffee and tea station. But style? Color? Location? Nope.

A growl similar to Rhys's rumbled in my chest. I needed to work on something, get my hands dirty, forget the frustrations of the day. I stalked to the studio area and found a blank canvas. Stripping my shirt, cranking up the music, and wrapping an apron around my waist in hopes of protecting my jeans, I set up my paints and brushes and submersed myself in a new piece.

How the fuck was this ever going to work out?

4

RHYS

I STOMPED up the stairs to my apartment, flung my clothes onto my bed, and pulled on shorts, a t-shirt, and running shoes. My contacts were drying out my eyes, so I exchanged them for a pair of glasses suited for running and fixed a thin rubber hair band on my head to keep my floppy blond hair from hanging in my face as I ran.

I was not much of a runner. I preferred yoga or a spin class or a few burpees. I only ran when I was pissed.

And I was pissed.

Yes, I'd run away from the studio in a huff. But the day had been overwhelmingly frustrating with Benji and I butting heads on nearly every single decision we needed to make. I had to take a break.

I shot down the stairs and onto the sidewalk. I pulled up a generic running playlist and popped in earbuds. The burn in my chest and legs set in almost immediately and it spurred my anger.

Who the fuck did Benji Silver think he was? Coming in

with his plans as if I didn't have my own plans. Silver rug, silver décor, silver this, silver that.

Each slap of my feet against the sidewalk echoed Silver, Silver, Silver. Each fiery hot breath I pulled into my lungs delivered yet another angry complaint about Benji.

By the time I reached a park area, I'd run out of steam. Yanking out my earbuds, I slowed to a walk and headed toward the little fish pond. I couldn't run any farther, I couldn't think about the shit show this business situation was turning into. I shouldn't have been able to think of Benji anymore either.

But I could.

And I was out of angry thoughts. Oh, they were still there, swirling in my head.

But my head and heart betrayed me by bringing to mind thoughts of Benji in my arms, Benji's mouth on mine, Benji in my bed moaning my name.

Holy fuck.

How could I want someone so badly yet be completely incapable of working with him?

Maybe you're not incapable of working with him. Maybe you're just being a brat. Maybe you're just looking for reasons why things wouldn't work between you two. Maybe you need to stop thinking everything has to be perfect.

Whether the voice in my head was mine, Caroline's, or a combination of the two, it pissed me off. Even considering a relationship with Benji when we couldn't even decide on a damn rug would be setting us up for complete and total disaster. And what of the business then?

"Golden, good to see you, man." A voice to my left pulled me from my thoughts.

"Triston, how's it going?" I slapped an old college buddy on the shoulder. We'd dated for a bit, but he'd had some family stuff going on and we ended up being better off as friends. Honestly, the craziness of some of his family issues made me worry about how stable a relationship between Triston and me could have ever been.

"Good, good. How's Caroline? How's the art?" Triston leaned against the railing that encircled the decorative pond.

"Caroline is good, neck deep in all of her philanthropy. Art is going well. In the middle of setting up a studio and display floor." I wiped sweat from my brow with the arm of my shirt.

"Dating? Thought I saw you at Metro the other night with a guy." Triston waggled his brow.

"Eh, was seeing someone for a while, but a lot of wrenches recently got thrown into the mix and it's probably not going to work out." I frowned and attempted to push down the sad feeling that filled my chest when I admitted that out loud. "How's your family?"

Triston laughed. "Still putting the fun in dysfunctional. Mom and Dad got back together. Gluttons for punishment. My sister had another baby. I've got six nieces and nephews now. My brother is dealing with some pretty heavy shit with his ex. Overall, we're just a big mess. But they're my mess and I love them."

I chuckled. "Your family are nice people, but those are the types of messes I'm determined to avoid. Perfect example of why the guy I was kinda seeing and I can't continue. I don't want to end up in situations like that." I gave Triston a nudge. "Don't get me wrong, I like your family, I just can't allow myself to get derailed by drama like that."

Triston raised a brow and studied me for a moment. "Nah, I don't look at it like that. We all make mistakes, none of us is perfect, *life* is far from perfect. But if you avoid imperfect relationships, you may miss out on the most perfect person for you. Imperfections are what make us real. And a *real* relationship will never be perfect." He glanced at his phone. "I gotta go. Holler at me some day, we'll grab lunch. And I definitely want to see this studio once it's up and running." He slapped me on the shoulder and jogged off.

I glanced to the left and to the right. Back to my apartment? Or to the studio? I opted for the studio. I could at least organize some supplies or something.

And maybe see Benji?

"Shut up," I muttered.

"…if you avoid imperfect relationships, you may miss out on the perfect person for you. Imperfections are what make us real. And a real relationship will never be perfect."

Triston's words played through my head over and over. And over.

I heard what he was saying.

It made sense. I believed it.

But for other people. Not for me.

Or at least not for Benji and me.

If we couldn't even set up a business without wanting to strangle each other, how would we work out a relationship? No, whatever had started to grow between us was doomed the moment Mr. Scott fucked up the lease.

Then why can't you get Benji out of your mind?

"Shut *up*," I growled through clenched teeth as I

reached the backdoor of the studio. I slid my key into the lock and slipped inside.

Benji was there. Oblivious to the world around him, earbuds in, paint brush in hand.

Jeans hugging his ass, no shirt, and looking sexy as hell as he worked.

Fuck.

I wanted to go back to before the lease situation screwed us over. Back to when things were tentative yet exciting as we grew to know and trust each other.

I wanted him back in my arms, back in my bed.

I wanted to watch movies with him, eat dinner with him, dance with him.

I missed holding him, missed talking with him, missed having him in my life.

He's still in your life.

Not how I want him to be.

Maybe not exactly the way you'd planned, but that doesn't mean it can't work.

I shook my head and leaned against the door to admire both his painting and his body. The colors, the strokes, the passion of the piece mesmerized me just as much as the strength in his broad shoulders, trim waist, and muscled arms. I recognized anger in the painting. Had he started it after I stormed out? But I also caught glimpses of hope and determination in his choice of colors and brush strokes. His initial anger had calmed and morphed into something brighter.

My initial anger had faded into a melancholy of mourning what might have been.

What could still be if Benji's work is any indication.

I gritted my teeth. "Shut. Up."

Benji turned and startled to find me standing in the studio. But his surprise quickly gave way to a smile.

Go to him.

I scowled as I pushed off of the door and slipped into the night. There was simply too much going on for me to consider trying to bring back whatever we might have had going between us.

As I crawled into bed that night, I thought of all the things Benji and I needed to discuss and work out. We wanted to open as soon as possible. I had some things I simply wouldn't budge on. But I knew Benji did as well. How the fuck were we ever going to get the studio and display floor up and running as a legitimate business and livelihood?

Maybe you'll need to think outside of your self-absorbed box for a bit.

I ran a hand over my face, rolled to my side, and buried my head under the pillow.

"Shut up," I whispered.

5

BENJI

"I SWEAR to God he's the most infuriating man I've ever met." I stabbed at a bite of waffle and swirled it in pool of butter and syrup before stuffing it in my mouth.

Bode snickered. "He's got you all kinds of riled up, huh?" He sipped his coffee.

Bode, Sage, Kyson, and I were seated at a corner table at Love Handle eating brunch before we headed out for our regular Sunday shopping trip.

"Well, we wanted to open this coming week, but it looks like that's not happening because we can't agree on *anything*." I shoved another bite of waffle in my mouth. "I think sometimes he just disagrees and causes an issue because he can and he knows it pisses me off."

"Dude, you need to relax. You've got a vein bulging in your head. Kyson, tell him he needs to relax." Bode put a hand on my shoulder. "For real, calm down. You have to work with him, best to get this all figured out and smooth out the ruffled feathers."

"What are you guys disagreeing on?" Sage asked before taking a bite of his breakfast sandwich.

"The list of what we're *not* disagreeing on is much shorter." I took a drink of orange juice.

Sage waited.

"We've agreed on the layout of our displays and pieces." I shrugged.

"That's it?" Kyson wiped his mouth with a napkin.

I nodded. "We both want a big area rug, coffee and tea station, decorative fixtures, a sales counter, but we can't agree on the color or location of any of it."

"Is it that you *can't* agree or just haven't given it enough effort?" Bode leaned on his elbows. "Sounds like maybe you both have these big, great ideas and plans and now you need to combine them and you're finding that hard." My brother held a hand up when I frowned. "I get it, completely. If I'd had to share The Salty Lizard and cooperate with someone else's ideas all of a sudden, I would have lost my damn mind."

Yeah, Bode would have likely exploded. A flutter of pride filled my chest that maybe I was handling it somewhat better than he would have.

"I'm thinking you both need to swallow some pride, open your minds more to the benefit of the business rather than holding former plans in clenched fists, discuss two or three top items that need decided. Maybe start with smaller negotiations. Once you can work through a coffee/tea station, maybe a bigger decision will be easier to cooperate on." Kyson poured another cup of coffee from the carafe and stirred a packet of raw cane sugar into the dark brew.

I sighed. "How much of a baby's ass do I sound like if I

say I don't want to swallow my pride or cooperate or negotiate?" My head was heavy in my hands as I leaned forward.

"It's a natural reaction." Sage squeezed my shoulder. "But if you dig deep and you're honest with yourself, you'll realize that the studio has a much better chance of being successful if you guys can come together and mesh your ideas. May end up being the best thing you've ever done and you'll look back on this time and laugh at all the drama."

I pursed my lips. "Yeah. Maybe." The level of doubt floating through my head was beginning to give me a headache.

We paid our bills and headed toward the bulk warehouse store. We'd learned quickly while living together that it was cheaper and easier to do the majority of our shopping with a once-a-month warehouse trip and just make quick trips to the local grocery for smaller items we didn't need a large supply of.

The four of us could have easily split up the list, gathered what we needed, met up to check out and cut time off of the trip. But our shopping trips had become something we all looked forward to. We stuck together, taking turns pushing the cart, trying samples, and pointing out items we should get even if they weren't on the list. These three men, my twin, my cousin, and Sage, were my best friends and I enjoyed our time together and didn't want to take it for granted.

But my mind kept flitting to Rhys.

Kyson and Sage moved farther down the condiment aisle, but Bode walked near me. "You really like him, huh?"

"What? Who?" I played dumb, my cheeks heating even as I spoke because there was no way to fool my brother.

He chuckled. "Remember when you guys rode me about admitting I liked Sage? Well, maybe you should take your own advice." He elbowed me. "Rhys, duh. That day he snuck out, you made it sound like it was super casual and not going anywhere. Was that a lie for our benefit or something you were trying to convince yourself of?"

I took a deep breath. Not exactly the conversation I wanted to have with my brother in the bulk warehouse store, but Bode was like a dog with a bone and I knew he wouldn't let it go. "The sex is absolutely amazing, like deeper than just physical. We were getting along great, had really interesting conversations, and I was really starting to like having him around. I enjoyed spending time with him. We hadn't labeled it as anything serious, but we were definitely moving from the casual hookup stage to more of a dating stage." A scowl pulled my brows together and intensified the dull ache in my head. "And then all of that was ripped away. We haven't talked about whatever we were doing before the building screw-up, we've only been butting heads about the studio."

Bode hummed. "What do you want?"

I laughed humorlessly. "I want to go back to the morning of Rhys sneaking out of my bed, the morning of the fateful phone call, and keep him in my bed, head off whatever paperwork fuck up took place, and have my own studio I can celebrate with a guy I was really starting to fall for."

Bode squeezed my neck. "Okay, let's focus on what we can control. If you and Rhys had gotten separate studio buildings you really would be kind of competitors. Sharing a building will take some adjusting, but you get to see him daily and spend time with him."

I snorted. "Spending time with him now is awkward and tense. Not exactly quality time."

Bode rolled his eyes. "Don't be obtuse. You know what I mean. Separate businesses would have likely been more of an obstacle to overcome. Sharing a building brings opportunities. Yes, it messes with your plans, but it also gives you the chance to grow whatever was starting between you two. It's awkward and tense now, but it doesn't have to be. You could be the bigger person, take a step toward making peace, extend an olive branch. And discuss the personal side of the relationship as well as the business side."

"Why do *I* have to be the one to bend and be the bigger person?" I huffed and ran a hand through my hair. "God, I hate the way I sound. I'm being a sniveling brat."

Bode put his arm around me and laughed. "Well, Rhys is too. So, it's not just you. But you can move from the negativity to something more positive. *If* you're willing to. Sure, Rhys could do the same. But you can't control him, may as well take the step to move things along."

I thought about Bode's words as we turned the corner to catch up with Kyson and Sage.

"So, the sex is good, huh?" Bode bumped his hip against mine.

I groaned. "So damn good. Like out of this world good. Maybe I've only been with shitty sex partners my whole life, I don't know. But everything with Rhys is better, deeper, hotter than any sex I've ever had."

Bode laughed. "I get it. Same with Sage. I've had some

ho-hum sex, and I've had really good sex. But things with Sage are off the charts."

I watched as Kyson and Sage discussed something intently in front of the cereals.

"Do you think Kyson and Bay will ever find their way to each other?" I'd seen the way my cousin and our friend, Bay, looked at each other. The four of us sometimes watched Bay's little boy, Arlo, when Bay couldn't get away from his motorcycle shop. Bay's sister had died and left Arlo to Bay; he was an amazing dad, but I saw the longing gazes between Kyson and Bay and wanted them to find happiness and fulfilment in each other.

Bode scrunched up his face. "Who knows. I don't think either of them would deny they are attracted to each other. But I think Bay is so focused on being a good dad and Kyson is deep in setting up his business. Neither of them seems to be the type for a quick one-and-done, and I'm not sure they are at a point where they can devote time to a relationship." He shrugged. "But, then again, I'm encouraging you to do just that while you're setting up your business. Maybe I should start in on Kyson too." He smiled. "I just want you guys as happy as I am with Sage."

"Oh, how things change," I teased and nudged Bode. He had fought tooth and nail before admitting he was attracted to the much younger Sage, but now they were in a solid, loving, sickeningly sweet relationship and I never passed up the opportunity to rib my twin about how much he'd kicked and screamed in protest of anything to do with Sage.

"Yeah, yeah." Bode grabbed Sage around the neck and kissed the top of his head. "I was slow on the uptake, but

I'm smarter now and all the better for it. Don't be like me. Make that first step."

Sage squawked but quickly relaxed into Bode's arms. "I don't know what you're talking about, but pick your cereal so we can be done."

We finished our shopping and checked out, loaded the truck, lugged the groceries up the stairs, and made quick work of putting everything away.

And the whole time, I couldn't stop thinking about Rhys.

That night, I stared at my phone for a full five minutes before finally gritting my teeth and tapping out a message to Rhys.

Me: *Extending an olive branch. Would like to invite you to a working lunch. Topics will include color schemes, locations of sales floor items, and studio name. You in?*

6

RHYS

I STARED at the text for a full five minutes.

Various thoughts and answer options crashed like waves in my head.

I could ignore the invitation.

Or I could flat out turn it down.

Neither of those options were going to help me or the studio.

I missed Benji. Even if we could only be business partners now, I didn't like the rift between us. I felt alone and miserable, I wanted him back in my life even if it wasn't exactly the way I wished it could be. And my art had suffered tremendously since the whole lease snafu.

But I didn't want to submit so easily.

Damn man, do you hear yourself? The guy seems to be trying and the invite seems genuine. Accepting it isn't submitting, it's making a move for the betterment of your studio. Get over your damn self.

I tapped out text reply.

Me: *Sounds like a plan. I'm in.*

I watched the little dots indicating Benji was typing.

Benji: *Great. How about lunch tomorrow? Get started early? 10:30? Where?*

Did I really want to have tense discussions with Benji at a public place? Although, on the flip side, maybe being in public would keep us on best behavior. No, we'd be more comfortable and productive in a personal environment. I glanced around my living room. I had plenty of space. We could spread out sketches of the studio, catalogs, our laptops, and get some real work done.

Me: *Let's do lunch at my place. We'll order in. Start at 9? Order lunch around 11? Bring your laptop, catalogs, notes, all that.*

Benji took forever to reply.

Shit. Maybe this was a bad idea. Did he not want to come to my place? I tossed my phone on the couch and grabbed a bottle of water. Should I text him and explain my reasoning for inviting him to my place? Did he think I was trying to get the upper hand? Start something back up?

I snatched up my phone, ready to tell him to forget it.

Benji: *That works. I'll be there at 9. I'm ready to bury this and get things up and running.*

I took a deep breath and smiled.

Me: *Same. See you tomorrow.*

I sighed. A short time ago, I would have been excited about making plans with Benji because it would have meant great company and conversation and amazing sex. These plans were exciting for a different reason, but my chest felt empty as I let go of whatever small thing may have been growing between Benji and me.

* * *

Benji knocked at exactly nine o'clock the next morning. I swung open the door and offered a tentative smile. "Good morning." I gestured toward the living room. "Figured we'd be most comfortable spread out here in the living room."

We set up our laptops, Benji plopped down a stack of catalogs, I tossed a notebook on the coffee table, and we both sat cross-legged on the floor.

"Okay, first decision," Benji began.

I swallowed thickly.

"What are we ordering for lunch?" Benji winked.

"What are you in the mood for?"

Benji appeared to think about it for a moment and I tried to ignore the way my stomach fluttered as I watched his beautiful face. "Big ol' burger?"

"Sounds good. Punch Burger?" I knew they had amazing burgers.

"Perfect." Benji grabbed a pen. "Okay, now we can get down to the nitty-gritty. Where do you want to start?"

"The name. I think we can't really feel like it's *our* place until we name it something we can both agree on." I tapped a pen against my knee before reaching for the notebook to make notes.

"What names did you have in mind when it was just you?"

"I was going to play on Golden or Gold. Golden Art, Studio Gold, The Gold Exchange, something along those lines." I shrugged. "Honestly, I wasn't *in love* with any of my ideas." I didn't like admitting that because it felt like I was giving Benji an opening to push his studio name on me.

"Well, as attached as I am to The Silver Creative, I can totally understand why you'd not be happy with that name." Benji pursed his lips. "But we can work with Silver and Gold. Or even Golden."

I doodled on my paper for a bit. Silver and Gold went together very well. "I think I like Gold, I've had people call me Golden and Gold most of my life. But Silver and Gold go together the best. People are used to hearing it like that."

"Silver and Gold Art. The Silver and Gold Exchange." Benji played with some of my original ideas.

"The Silver and Gold Creative." I said the words and immediately knew it was perfect. Damn it. I didn't *want* it to be perfect, but it was.

"The Silver and Gold Creative." Benji tested the name on his tongue before glancing my way. "Thoughts?"

"As much as I hate to admit it, I love it." I shrugged. "Damn it, I really love it."

Benji smiled wryly. "We can keep brainstorming, I'm not against coming up with something completely different."

"What do you think about The Silver and Gold Creative?" Maybe he wouldn't like the alteration of his original name.

"I kinda love it." Benji's cheeks flushed. "But I don't want to make you feel like you're just an extra addition to my original name."

I thought about it. "No, I really do like the name. Silver and Gold go together easily and the words are almost always listed silver and gold rather than gold and silver. I like it and I'm on board if you are." I raised a brow.

Benji smiled and nodded. "Yeah, I really like it. I'm in."

I stuck out my hand. "Welcome to The Silver and Gold Creative."

Benji took my hand and shook. "Thank you."

I ignored the electric heat that jumped through my body when our skin touched. "Mark the calendar. Benji and Rhys just made a decision. Together. With no blood shed."

"Tis a monumental occasion, but let's not celebrate prematurely. We've got about a million other decisions to make." Benji nudged me with his elbow.

But after that first agreement, everything else seemed to fall into place.

"Okay, so I was thinking of a silver rug. You wanted gold." Benji raised his brows.

"So, we find a silver and gold rug." My face relaxed into a genuinely relieved smile.

We flipped through catalogs and looked up item numbers online. Within twenty minutes we'd found the perfect silver and gold floor rug for the display floor.

"This will look amazing with the hardwood floors." Benji rubbed his hands together. "Okay, what's next?"

"Fixtures?"

He rolled his eyes. "This is getting too easy. Duh, we do a mixture of brushed silver and gold fixtures."

I laughed. "Duh."

By eleven, we'd ordered an eclectic mix of silver and gold fixtures that we agreed would mesh well to represent the melding of our names and our artwork.

"Lunch?" Benji stretched. "Then we tackle the most important item."

"The coffee and tea station," we both said at the same time and chuckled.

My heart clenched a bit. Being with Benji, laughing, enjoying his company, was so nice. But it also hurt because it was something that could go no further.

Do you know for sure that it can't? Maybe you should talk to him about it.

I shook away the thought. Our studio was more important than a relationship. I pulled up the Punch Burger site and we placed our orders.

We each immersed ourselves in our phones while we waited for lunch to arrive. It was a comfortable silence. Once the food arrived, we ate and made small talk about Benji's brother's bar, The Salty Lizard, and Kyson's massage therapy practice.

"I definitely plan to set up an appointment with him. Love a good massage." I shoved a fry in my mouth. "Do you get freebies?"

Benji winked. "I may get a family discount. It's nice."

We cleaned up our lunch mess.

"Ready to hit it again?" I cracked my knuckles.

"Let's do it." Benji pulled up a search page on his laptop. "We'll need a silver and gold theme for the coffee and tea station."

Within an hour we'd gathered together the perfect mix of silver and gold coffee and tea supplies and accessories. We'd grabbed onto the theme of meshing the color theme and our different artistic styles together in a way that worked and it felt good to plan and order and prepare for the studio's opening.

"Let's contact local businesses to see if we can get daily treats from them. A different offering each day. Should be good advertising for them and maybe they can do a little *Featured At The Silver and Gold Creative* promo for us in their shops." I wrote some notes as Benji started a list of places we could contact.

An hour later, we'd emailed our top ten choices. Once we'd heard back from them, we'd set up a schedule for which days each would be the featured treat at the studio.

We shut our laptops, organized our supplies, and leaned back against the couch with huge sighs.

"Wow, that was exhausting, but it feels really good to have it done." Benji turned his head toward me.

When I turned my head toward him, we were only inches apart. Those striking hazel eyes, gorgeous face, and kissable lips set me on fire. I wanted to lean in, capture his mouth, pull him close, and never let go.

My heart nearly leapt from my chest when Benji's hand on the floor grazed against me, his pinky against mine. Was the touch on purpose? Did Benji still want me the same way I still wanted him?

A bing sounded from one of our phones and broke the moment.

Benji coughed and picked up his phone. "We've got some emails back."

We spent a few minutes discussing particulars regarding the studio before Benji sighed. "Guess I better head out. Let's set a tentative opening date. Do a whole grand opening weekend. I'll have Kyson and Bode advertise at their places. I bet Bay would spread the word at his shop. Let's make a list of businesses on and around Mass. Ave. We'll split it up and stop in to see if they'll put up flyers for us. I'll get one made up and printed."

I frowned.

"No worries, I'll clear it with you first. Promise." Benji winked. "Okay, so we've got our homework and a plan. You feel good about this?"

We stood up. "Yeah, a lot better now than before." I followed Benji to the door.

He turned suddenly and faced me. "Can I ask you something?"

I nodded, my throat suddenly dry.

"If this screw-up hadn't happened, would we have kept up whatever we were doing?" His forehead wrinkled.

I thought about his question. "Honestly? Probably not. Maybe we would have tried, but we would have ended up as competing studios, super busy, probably would have drifted apart." I was pretty confident in that answer.

"And now?" Benji's words were soft.

Tell him you want something to continue. Tell him you miss him, want him.

I took a deep breath. "Not *exactly* competitors now, but still swamped and need to focus on the studio. Right?"

You fucking coward.

My heart hurt. Why couldn't I just be honest with him?

Benji's lips pressed into a thin line. "Yeah, the studio is important. Glad we got a lot of work done today and didn't kill each other." He smiled slightly, but it seemed fake.

Benji turned and walked out the door.

I wanted to call him back and tell him I was lying. Pull him into my arms, kiss him, take him to bed. But we had a business to run. What happened if an intimate relationship crashed and burned? Where would The Silver and Gold Creative be after that? As much as I missed what Benji and I had, it felt important to focus on the future of our business. The studio was to be our livelihood, it would take hard work to keep it up and running. A relationship would bring great sex and companionship, but that wouldn't pay the bills.

Besides, Benji could have protested, told me that he wanted to keep up whatever we'd had going. But he didn't.

So, it seemed we were on the same page.

7

BENJI

"SO, wait. You asked him if he wanted to keep things going and he straight up said no?" Bode frowned a few days later as I filled them in on my working lunch with Rhys. "Are you sure?" He and Sage cuddled on the couch.

I shrugged. "I mean, I didn't spill my guts or flay open my heart to tell him how badly I wanted that, but I gave him a chance to say he was interested and he didn't. I guess maybe what we had meant a little more to me than to him."

"You kinda let on that you wanted it to continue and asked him what he thought? What did he say?" Kyson asked from his place on the recliner as he took a big bite of cereal.

I huffed. After a few days of playing the scene between Rhys and me over in my head, I came to my best friends to whine and bitch and commiserate, but they weren't commiserating, they were giving me the third degree as if Rhys turning me down was my fault. "I asked him if the lease screw-up hadn't happened if he thought we would have kept going with whatever we had. He said probably not because we would have become competitors and been busy with our own studios." I took a breath. "So, like an idiot, I asked 'What about now?'"

"And?" Sage asked.

"He replied, 'Not *exactly* competitors now, but still swamped and need to focus on the studio. Right?' What was I supposed to say to that?" I took the last bite of cereal and stood to take my bowl to the sink. "Like, he says we need to focus on the studio and I'm supposed to what? Throw myself at him and beg to go back to what we *might* have had? I liked him, the sex was amazing, but things weren't *perfect* so maybe I'm putting too much stock in what we maybe had. I gave him the perfect opportunity to say he wanted to keep seeing me." I tossed my bowl in the sink with a clatter.

"And he gave *you* the perfect opportunity to say that you wanted to keep seeing him." Kyson was giving me a look that screamed *Duh!* when I returned to the living room.

I scoffed. "Yeah, telling me we'll be swamped and need to focus on the studio is a great opening for me to say I want more than that." I ran a hand over my face. "I need to get over him and throw myself into my art."

"Do we need to spell it out?" Bode asked. "Dude, if he said 'need to focus on the studio, *right*?' then that's the perfect opportunity to disagree, say you want something more."

I started to protest, but clamped my mouth shut. *Shit.* Were they right? I shook my head. "No, Rhys isn't the type to play games and be coy." I said the words, but I wasn't one-hundred percent sure of them. Rhys never came across as unsure of himself when we were together, especially not in bed and conversations.

But then again, I hadn't realized how *not* confident he was in his work until we got thrown into sharing a studio. Maybe he wasn't as sure of himself as I'd thought. Did he say what he said in hopes that I would disagree and give him an opening? Did he want things back to the way they were before?

"You've never really been one to play games, either." Kyson pointed at me. "I think you both like each other, want to be together, are fearful the other doesn't want it as bad, and are using the studio as your excuse to break up before anything can get too serious."

I huffed, but really had no words. I picked up my phone and stuffed it in my pocket. "I'm going to the studio for last minute prep before the opening. You guys can all come at some point this weekend, yeah?"

"Wouldn't miss it." Bode pulled Sage closer to his side and kissed his head. "We'll be there throughout the weekend. Proud of you."

"Thanks. Oh," I snapped my fingers, "were you able to put up any flyers?" I'd spent a day earlier in the week creating a flyer for The Silver and Gold Creative grand opening. Rhys had shocked me by saying he thought it looked great. Had a bunch printed and gave a few to the guys to share. Rhys and I had hung them in as many nearby businesses, libraries, and community spaces as we could find.

"I put some up in the student union and library on campus. There's also a few community happenings boards around campus so I hung them on there too." Sage smiled shyly as Bode and Kyson nodded that they'd done their part with the flyers.

"Thanks so much. Rhys shared a Facebook page with me, I'll send it to you. Maybe you could share that too?" I kinda felt bad asking them to help so much, but I knew they didn't mind and wanted to help. "He's got a website going, we're going to keep adding to it. He set up Twitter, Instagram, and Facebook."

"Send it all to us, we'll share it all. I'll shout you out from The Salty Lizard social media pages as well as from my personal ones." Bode stood from the couch and roughed me up. "I know an art studio opening may not be as loud and obnoxious as a bar opening, but I think this will be a good weekend."

We said our casual goodbyes and I headed to the studio. My plan was to create for a while and then do some last-minute things to get ready for the grand opening.

When I walked into the back room, I had to force myself to breathe. Rhys was deep in concentration, his face covered as he wielded the welding gun over his latest piece. My eyes appreciated the artistic work before being drawn to the way his jeans clung to his legs and ass. His broad chest and strong arms were definitely visible under his plain black t-shirt.

My mind traveled back to one night we were cuddled in his bed. Our skin was damp with sweat, the room heavy with sex, but we'd finally caught our breaths and started laughing about stupid stuff we'd done as kids. We spent the next couple hours swapping stories of our youth and nothing had ever felt more natural or perfect.

I never knew how people would react when they found

out Kyson, Bode and I were each other's first sexual encounters, but Rhys had listened, tossed the idea around for a moment and then nodded. "Really, if people took the time to think about it, it makes complete sense. The three of you were as close as any three kids could be. You trusted each other, you had these curiosities, what better way to explore than with people you know and love?"

Now I watched Rhys immersed in his work and wished once again we could go back to those amazingly close and comfortable conversations after sex. Yes, most of our great talks were after sex, but I could totally see us expanding to dinner and movie dates in addition to spectacular sex.

My ass clenched and my dick took notice as I continued to creep on Rhys and recall the sex we'd shared. He was so gorgeous and smart and overall a good guy. Did he have some self-absorbed issues? Sure. But I did too. None of us were perfect. I missed the time we spent together. Maybe I just missed being with someone.

I watched Rhys while I thought over that. I missed sex, I missed being with someone, but it wasn't just that. I missed *Rhys*. Were we at that point of adulting where we had to push aside our wishes and desires in order to take care of the important things?

Rhys looked up and froze.

I smiled and waved. "Looks good." Yeah, outwardly I meant the artwork. I wished he could know that I meant he looked good as well.

"I don't really like being watched." Rhys frowned and glanced at his piece of work.

I tensed immediately. "Sorry." I held up my hands. "We now share a studio if you haven't noticed. I'll be here a lot. Just like I expect you will. I'm sorry for appreciating your work." I watched him for a moment longer. "Promise not to *steal* it," I sneered. *God, I hated what this whole situation had done to Rhys and me, and I hated the way it had me acting.*

"Exactly why we should have divided up the studio so we'd both have separate, *private* workspaces." Rhys wiped a bit of sweat from his brow with a cloth. "This shit isn't going to work."

"Look, I was enjoying watching you work. The piece looks great, like always. No way I'm copying off you. One, I'm not that type of person. Two, if I tried what you do, it would just be a big glob. Chill the fuck out. Let's give it a bit. If we find we can't work around each other, we'll hang curtain dividers or put up walls." I gestured toward the ceiling. "I just hate to lose the openness of the space."

Rhys gave a quick nod, pulled his protective eye gear back in place and went back to working.

I growled under my breath and headed to my pottery work station. I had several pieces at various stages of painting, glazing, and firing. I hadn't used the wheel since moving into this studio and I was itching to get my hands into some clay. But I wasn't in the mood right then. Probably for the best, wouldn't want Rhys stealing my ideas. I snorted quietly to myself. What the actual fuck? We made completely different types of art, and even if we didn't, I'd have no fear of him copying me and no plans to copy him. Surely his behavior just now had stemmed from his insecurity in his work and maybe nerves about the opening.

I shook my head as I set to work painting pieces ranging from earrings to vases to pots to coffee mugs. The nerves, I totally got. I was nervous about the opening. I was scared shitless that six months from now we'd be faced with closing. Or worse, and it wasn't even something I'd allowed in my head until just that moment, I'd have to leave the studio to Rhys because he was doing great, but I was failing. A few sales of large pieces for him could keep him going for a month or so. If I only sold a coffee mug and earrings here and there, I'd be screwed. So, yeah. I understood the nerves.

But I didn't get his insecurity in his work. First, he always seemed so confident and self-assured when talking about his art. Second, he was so damn talented. How could he not see that?

Maybe the confidence is a façade. Now that he's faced with you seeing his work from conception to display floor, he's feeling raw and vulnerable.

I shrugged. Yeah, I could see that. We both needed some great interest in our art, some crazy good sales, and lots of customers coming in and also spreading the word to give us that boost of confidence and assuredness in this venture.

For the first time, I realized just how stressed Bode had felt when he was opening The Salty Lizard and probably every day since. Owning your own business was *not* for the faint of heart. And putting your work out there for all to see was even worse.

I definitely could empathize with Rhys. *If* all of that was the actual reason for his shitty attitude. But if he kept up his asshole routine, I wasn't sure I could feel too bad for him or try to understand where he was coming from.

Maybe the two of us would learn quickly that we were best off to be in the space together, but not try to mesh our work, our sales, or our talents.

* * *

An hour later, I wasn't even sure being in the space together was going to work. We'd gone from disagreeing on everything, to a productive working lunch and tentative truce, to now being snippy and snarky about everything.

Every.

Thing.

Honestly, I was thinking we should maybe make up a schedule so we could be at the studio and avoid each other being there all together. I could work Monday, Wednesday, Friday, and half of Sunday. Rhys could work Tuesday, Thursday, Saturday, and the other half of Sunday.

I seriously contemplated bringing up the idea, but Rhys seemed to be biting my head off at every suggestion, and no doubt he'd think it was a devious plan to sell millions on my days alone in the studio.

I sighed.

Actually, if I was being honest—and no way was I willing to admit it—I was being just as snippy with him. Did it really matter that he'd put the sugar in a gold piece with a silver spoon when I'd planned to put the sugar in a silver piece with a gold spoon? No. No, it did not. But I'd gotten huffy over it anyway.

"I thought the gold knobs would be best on that corner cabinet." Rhys folded his arms over his chest.

I took a deep breath and glanced toward the cabinet. "The silver ones look nice. We can't hodge-podge the pieces all over the place. We need to look like we've got a plan and some sort of artistic eye. You know, since we're *artists* trying to sell art?"

"Agreed. But why are you making all the decisions? Did we discuss which knobs were going on which fixtures?"

"No, I didn't think to ask. I was probably busy wondering why you automatically stuck the sugar in the gold container instead of asking me where I wanted it." I could have only sounded more childish if I'd stomped my foot and stuck out my tongue along with my tiny tirade.

Rhys huffed. "Are you about ready to call it a day? We've got about thirty minutes of work left to do. I say we finish it, go home, and get some rest to be ready for tomorrow."

"Or maybe you just want me to go home so you can have the place to yourself? Maybe redo a bunch of the work I've done today to fit what *you* want?" I narrowed my eyes.

Holy shit. Rhys had me acting as paranoid as he was.

Rhys ran a hand over his face. "Look, we're both nervous and clearly cranky. You take three gold items and I'll take three silver items. We spread them out on the display floor in a way that looks good and then we go home. I need a breather."

"Crabby toddlers need their naps, huh?" I smirked. "Yeah, I could use a break. We've got this place as set up and ready as possible." I held my hand out and took the three gold items.

Thirty minutes later, Rhys and I stood in the middle of the room. We were still snippy, still snarky, still grumpy. Definitely still nervous. But the place looked amazing. There was nothing else to do except wait for the grand opening tomorrow and cross our fingers that customers, *buying* customers, showed up.

I gave a reluctant nod of my head. Rhys returned the gesture. We moved toward the back door. I felt like I should say something inspirational on the eve of our big business venture's opening. But Rhys just pushed open the back door and turned toward his place.

With a sigh and a shrug, I did the same.

* * *

"Dude, the place looks amazing," Bode clapped me on the back and spoke lowly in my ear, "but you and Rhys need to try to at least *appear* to be business partners. It feels very divided in here. Not the displays so much, but the vibe between you two is *not* pulling in browsers and buyers." My twin elbowed me. "Suck it up, Buttercup. No one is going to want to be in here, let alone purchase pieces or come back if they get an uncomfortable, hostile vibe. Share his work, introduce him to friends and customers, talk him up, present a united front."

When I started to protest, Bode held up a hand. "I get it. He's being just as big of a baby's ass as you are. But instead of both of you pouting that things didn't go your way, smile and be a big boy. People need to see that this is a partnership, a beautiful blending of two artists and their work. You have to sell them on same but different. You and Rhys are similar but very different. Your work is different but has some definite similarities. You have to make it look like this was all put together for a reason and not just because of a goof-up." Bode leaned in again. "If he's not going to take the first step, you need to. For the benefit of your studio. Fake it 'til you make it if you need to, but plaster on a smile and go sell these people on Rhys and Benji, on same but different, on The Silver and Gold Creative."

I took a deep breath, mulled over Bode's words for a moment, and then smiled wryly. "Damn, you'd actually make a really good motivational speaker." I nudged him with my hip. "Fine. I'll do it. But if he doesn't jump on board, I'm really not sure how long this place will survive."

Bode glanced toward where Rhys was standing with his older sister and chuckled. "From the look on his sister's face, Rhys is about to get the same speech." He shivered. "But I'm not sure she'll be as nice as I was."

I moved away from Bode and began to chat with customers. I kept an eye on Caroline and Rhys. Once they appeared to be done speaking, I'd grab Rhys and we could work the room. *Together.* I wasn't against this plan. Bode knew how to win people over, that was for sure. I just hoped Rhys wouldn't be too resistant and give me a reason to want to strangle him.

Let's be real, you just want any and every reason to kiss him. Maybe he'll give you that.

I snorted and covered it by clearing my throat. Rhys most definitely did *not* seem to want anything to do with kissing me anymore. I pushed down the hurt and turned my smile up to mega-watt level.

8

RHYS

"SMILE," Caroline purred in my ear, "and listen closely. You, my dear little brother, are being an absolute spoiled brat. Like a child asked to share his toy, or a brother jealous when his sibling gets more attention." She curled her arm into the crook of my elbow. "Keep smiling, don't let on that I'm giving you the angry mom treatment."

I plastered a smile on my face and chuckled as I whispered. "As long as you don't dig your nails into my arm like Mom used to, I'll play along."

Through a blinding stage smile, Caroline continued, "Oh, you'll do more than play along. You and Benji are filling this place with unwelcoming, almost hostile, vibes. You need to fix it *now*. Mingle with him, introduce him to people, show off his work, talk him up."

I took in a breath to protest.

"No, there is no argument on this one. Today, this weekend, is very important to your business. If people don't feel welcome and comfortable, they won't come back. No one needs to know you two were forced together because of a mistake. The entire place *looks* amazing and so very well meshed together. You both did an amazing job."

"Thanks," I mumbled.

"But none of that matters one single iota if you and Benji are giving off such negative, pouty, and divided vibes."

"But," I began.

"No buts." Caroline made as if she was straightening my collar and picking lint from my sleeve. "You're going to glue yourself to Benji's side. If I'm not mistaken, that gorgeous twin of his just gave him the same speech I'm giving you. So, push aside your self-absorbed selfishness for a bit and make this work." She moved directly in front of me and held me by my shoulders. "Your work is amazing and it *will* sell, but you and Benji have to do more than co-exist, you have to be true partners."

My gut twisted. *Business* partners. We needed to be business partners. Then why did my heart flip-flop at the thought of Benji and I being partners in other ways? Business, friendship, love. I wanted them all. But did I even know how to do any of those?

My sister leaned in to kiss my cheek. "And you two really need to be honest with each other about whatever it is that's still brewing between you. It may be just under the surface and somewhat easy to ignore for now. But sooner or later, all of those wants and desires and feelings will come bubbling to the surface and make a big mess if you're not prepared to handle them."

I took a deep breath. Seemed as if getting the business

partner part figured out and perfected was the top priority. I could keep pushing down the others. For now. I nodded at Caroline and walked toward Benji.

He met me halfway and took my hand with a smile on his face. Whether it was forced or not, I didn't know. But his touch and smile helped me relax slightly.

Before we had a moment to tackle the room together, Bode and Caroline were beside us shaking hands.

"Bode Silver, Benji's twin." Bode was definitely a people person as was evident in his genuine, relaxed, welcoming smile.

"Caroline Golden-Phipps, Rhys's sister." Caroline was well-practiced in meeting, greeting, and socializing.

"What are we going to do with these two?" Bode winked and crossed his arms across his chest as he smirked at his brother.

Caroline nodded. "I was *just* thinking the same thing." She glanced between Benji and me. "I really hope you boys will grow up and confront the feelings you've got for each other. But, most importantly for now, I hope you'll work this room and show off your art." She turned to Bode. "Introduce me to that beautiful man you walked in here with."

Bode held out his elbow and Caroline took the crook of his arm as they walked away.

Benji snorted. "I wonder if she means Sage or Kyson."

I glanced down to where our hands remained joined. My heart was as warm as the heat of that simple touch. "Well, she easily could be referring to either of them."

Benji nodded. "You ready to do this?"

I squeezed his hand. "Yeah."

We reluctantly let go of each other's hand before moving to one of the larger groups of visitors. Almost immediately, we fell into a very surprising but natural rhythm of introductions, small talk, speaking highly of each other's work, and then elaborating on our own work a bit.

Within an hour, my cheeks hurt from smiling so much, and the random squeeze from Benji's hand before we'd approach another customer or group gave me a thrill each time we touched.

About forty-five minutes before the first day's opening was scheduled to close, Benji pulled me to the rug in the middle of the display floor. He cleared his throat and began to speak as he took my hand.

"My partner, Rhys, and I wanted to thank you all for coming out to support The Silver and Gold Creative today. Just as Rhys and I have a lot of similarities and differences, so does our artwork. We want this studio to be a place that encourages and celebrates those similarities and differences in ourselves, our work, others, and our community."

Benji's palm was sweaty in mine, but that was the only clue that he was nervous as he spoke so eloquently. I squeezed his hand and cleared my throat.

"If you wish to purchase any artwork today, please see myself or Benji." I smiled and hoped I didn't look as awkward as I felt. "If not, please continue to browse. We'll be open this weekend as well, so please stop by. We'd love to see you all here as regulars to enjoy the coffee, tea, treats, and, of course, the art. And be sure to watch for Benji's art lesson schedule. He'll be teaching a variety of topics for all ages."

The crowd gave a small, quiet round of applause before returning to their browsing.

"Thank you," Benji whispered. "That meant a lot."

I shrugged. "After you talked up my work so much, it felt like the right thing to do."

We mingled with a few guests until Benji was pulled away to help with the purchase of a set of mugs.

"You two almost made that look fun."

I turned to find a man who looked so much like Benji and Bode that he *had* to be their cousin, Kyson. I smiled. "It actually was fun."

"I'm Kyson. The cousin." He held out his hand.

"Rhys. The," I paused and frowned, "business partner?"

Kyson laughed. "If that's the best you can come up with, it'll work. For now. But I think you and Benji are the only two people who don't see how badly you have it for each other." Kyson glanced toward the door and I heard the audible intake of his breath. "Nice meeting you. Come into Mass. Ave. Massage for a free session sometime," he mumbled before beelining straight for the door to greet the super-hot silver-fox who had just entered.

* * *

Benji and I cleaned up and organized after the last customer left. As I took the trash out, a thought ran on a continual link through my head like a damn freight train. We needed to talk. I *wanted* to talk. I wasn't ready to give up on whatever had barely had time to get started between us. But that meant swallowing my pride and admitting my insecurities, talking about feelings, and being vulnerable.

I didn't *want* to do any of those things.

But I did want Benji back in my life as more than just a business partner.

Or I at least wanted to give whatever we might have had a chance.

I ran a hand over my face and breathed deeply.

Did he feel anything close to the jumble of emotions I was feeling?

I stood at the backdoor and stared at it for several moments. Finally, with a phrase my dad used to say echoing in my head—"You gotta risk it if you want the biscuit."—I yanked open the door and found Benji in the front wrapping up the few leftover pastries.

He turned and smiled. "I don't think we should put these out again tomorrow. Want to take them home?"

I swallowed my fear. "Yeah, they'll be perfect for dessert."

Benji's face fell briefly, but he immediately covered it with a soft smile. "Have someone coming for dinner?"

I glanced down at his fashionable shoes and cleared my throat. "Was hoping you'd come over for dinner." I forced my eyes to meet his. "Maybe we could talk? Clear the air? Figure some things out?"

Benji's chest expanded as he took a deep breath and a sparkle shone from his eyes.

"Unless you don't think we have anything to talk about or figure out?"

He shook his head. "No, I'd love to talk and sort some things out. Can I bring anything?"

I wanted so badly to tell him to bring an overnight bag, but that seemed premature and presumptuous. "No. We'll order pizza or something. I've got beer and hard cider. Bring wine if you want some. Dessert is provided." I gestured toward the pastries and winked.

Benji nodded. "Okay. I'm going to swing by home, shower and change, and then I'll be over. Forty-five minutes?"

"Perfect." I wanted to pull him to me and hug him, but I just followed him out the backdoor.

We mumbled our goodbyes.

My heart thudded in my chest. Could I be open and honest with him? Could Benji do the same? Would we find we were on the same page? Or had our chance slipped away?

As I drove home, I thought about our circumstances. Yes, being forced to share the building had been a shock and not what we wanted to do. But if I'd had my own studio and Benji had his own, would we have been able to keep up any sort of relationship? Would we have even wanted to? We would have been true competitors. Would we have put forth the effort to continue?

Maybe being forced together was a blessing in disguise? Sure, it sucked at first. Knocked us on our asses and threw us for a real loop. But maybe we were finding our feet and getting a chance to give *us* a shot.

I gave the apartment a quick straightening, threw all the laundry in the washer, lit a couple candles, and changed the sheets. Just in case.

I was giddy with anticipation as I jumped in the shower. As hot water pelted my face, I forced myself to bring it down a few notches. Maybe Benji would prefer to just lay to rest whatever we'd had before, patch up our business partnership, work towards being just friends. The thought was a gut-punch, but I knew I needed to be prepared for the possibility.

9

BENJI

I RAN UP THE STAIRS, said a quick hello to Bode and Sage, and quickly shut myself in the bathroom. I rummaged through the cabinet and came up victorious with an enema kit. Was I likely being *very* presumptuous? Yes. But I was one to err on the side of caution; better safe than sorry.

I took care of business and jumped in the shower. Fifteen minutes later, I stood in front of my closet full of clothes and ran a towel through my dark hair. Would it be poor form to wear sweats and a t-shirt? We weren't going *out*. I was tired and ready to just be comfortable.

I shrugged and shimmied into a pair of sexy, orange mesh underwear, pulled on a soft gray shirt and a nicer pair of casual, straight-legged sweatpants. I knew I was possibly setting myself up for a huge letdown, but I tossed a toothbrush, deodorant, razor, and a pair of underwear into a backpack. Even if I spent the night, I'd need to come home to get dressed before heading to the studio tomorrow.

Cracking the door of my room, I listened for Bode or Sage. It wasn't that I didn't want to talk to them, but I was in a hurry to get to Rhys's place. The living room and kitchen appeared quiet. Bode and Sage had either gone to their room or down to The Salty Lizard. I crept out of my room and pulled the door shut.

As I tiptoed through the living room behind the couch like a kid trying to sneak out of the house, two heads popped up from the couch.

"Gotcha!" Bode grabbed my arm over the back of the couch.

I jumped and cursed.

Sage and Bode laughed.

"What the fuck are you two doing? You almost gave me a damn heart attack." I shifted the backpack on my shoulder and hoped they wouldn't notice it.

No such luck.

Bode chuckled. "Well, you made enough noise digging in the bathroom cabinet to rival a fucking herd of racoons. So, we assumed you were possibly prepping for a rendezvous with Rhys. We decided to hide and see if you attempted to sneak out. The backpack you're so adorably trying to hide makes me think we were right. Overnight at Rhys's place? What changed?"

"It's actually a gaze of racoons." Sage, on his knees next to Bode on the couch, hooked his arm through my brother's elbow.

Bode glanced at him, shook his head, and kissed Sage hard. "Fuck, I love you. For so many reasons, but partly because you're a fucking genius."

Sage blushed, but looked to me. "Did you and Rhys fix things?"

I lifted a shoulder. "Not sure." I blushed thinking they knew I'd prepped for possible sex. Oh well, they did the same. It's why we bought enema kits in bulk. "Rhys invited me over for dinner. Says he wants to talk and figure things out." I moved the backpack on my shoulder. "I may be being too hopeful, but I'd rather be prepared."

Bode pulled me against the back of the couch and hugged me from his kneeling position on the cushions. "That's great. I hoped you two would pull your heads from your asses and give yourselves a chance."

"We'll see what happens."

"Just be honest with each other. Tell him how you feel and what you want." Bode slapped me on the back. "We won't wait up." He winked and I laughed.

"If Sage starts sharing his knowledge of collective nouns, you'll probably be too busy fucking him senseless all night." I waggled my brows and gave a little wave as I turned to leave.

As I headed toward the door, I heard Sage.

"A pandemonium of parrots, a wisdom of wombats, an ambush of tigers, a shrewdness of apes."

I could just picture him murmuring in Bode's ear as he teased my brother with his random knowledge of what to call groups of animals.

"Fuck. To the bedroom *now*. You are so damn fuckable."

Bode must have thrown Sage over his shoulder because as I slipped on my sneakers, Sage shrieked in laughter and soon Bode's door slammed shut.

I laughed. I was so happy for Bode and Sage. They were together because Bode finally admitted he wanted Sage. Of course, they had different obstacles than Rhys and I had, but they were together because they worked through their issues.

I wanted Kyson and Bay to be together. Maybe they could work through their challenges.

Maybe Rhys and I could work out things and figure out what might be growing between us.

Arriving at Rhys's place about five minutes later, I tossed the backpack in the trunk. I'd come down and get it if I needed it. Showing up at his door with an overnight bag could definitely cause awkward vibes.

I stood outside Rhys's door and rubbed a sweaty palm on my pants with the pastries in the other hand. Taking a deep breath first, I blew it out and knocked.

He opened the door with a smile, his face flushed.

I took in his clothes and noted he'd dressed similarly to me. "Glad to see we had the same thought in dressing for comfort." I walked past him and put the pastries in the kitchen. I wanted to hug him, pull him close, bury my face in his neck and just breathe him in. Instead, I stood awkwardly.

Luckily, there was a knock at the door.

"Pizza." Rhys went to the door and returned with two boxes. "I got just cheese and loaded. Wasn't sure what you'd be in the mood for." He walked past me and went into the living room. "Bring whatever you want to drink. I'll take a beer, please."

I loved that Rhys seemed comfortable with me being there, but I was so nervous about our talk and whatever might happen, I wasn't sure I could stomach any food. I grabbed Rhys a beer and myself a hard cider.

By the time we'd each nibbled a piece of pizza and drained our drinks, I was about to jump out of my skin.

"You want to clean this up for now and talk? Eat later if we're hungry?" Rhys raised a brow.

I nodded and launched myself from the couch to gather the boxes and empty bottles. Rhys picked up the napkins and plates.

"These in the fridge or on the counter for now?" I held up the boxes.

Rhys was rinsing the beer and cider bottles at the sink. He gestured with his chin toward the counter. "There's good for now."

As if my body and heart were acting completely out of accordance with what my head said was a good idea, I moved close to Rhys, standing behind him and pressing my front against his back as he dried his hands on a towel.

He froze.

"I am completely on board with talking and figuring this out," I whispered against his ear, "but I need you to know that I've missed this, I've missed *you*, and I'm dying to kiss you." I trailed my lips along his neck and relished in the shiver that traveled through him.

Rhys turned and wrapped his arms around my waist. "Set a timer. We kiss for five minutes. Then we talk."

I slid my phone from my pocket and set the timer a split second before Rhys walked me backwards. When my back hit the wall, he cupped his hands around my face and stared at me for a moment.

I couldn't breathe. I needed him, I wanted him.

Rhys groaned before devouring my mouth. Our lips met with a hot spark and I savored the familiar flavor of him. I whimpered and opened my mouth. When his tongue brushed against mine, I thought my knees were going to give out.

I rolled my hips against his and enjoyed the hitch in Rhys's breathing. His cock was as hard as mine and the heat from his arousal seeped through my pants. The mesh underwear I'd chosen did nothing to stop the spread of pre-cum as I continued to rock our dicks together. I knew my sweatpants would have a wet spot.

I palmed Rhys's cock and mumbled against his mouth. "I want to suck you, choke on you, swallow everything you can give me."

Rhys groaned and kissed me, thrusting his tongue deep.

Beep-beep-beep.

We pulled apart with a moan.

"Fuck." Rhys adjusted himself. "Maybe we talk after."

I chuckled. "I think we should talk first. Clear the air and all that. Then we have all the time in the world."

Rhys rested his forehead against mine and sighed. "Fine. But I need to calm myself down for a minute. You can use the guest bathroom if you need." He grabbed two waters. "Two minutes."

Two minutes later, we settled on the couch and chugged our water.

"You okay with me going first?" Rhys screwed the lid back onto his bottle.

I nodded.

When I thought he'd start talking, he just sat there.

I waited.

"Why is this so hard? Does it seem weird that we've been intimately close, but I have so much trouble finding the words to tell you how I'm feeling?" Rhys took another drink of water.

"You mean that it seems odd we've eaten each other's

ass, but talking about feelings and emotions and what we want is difficult?"

Rhys snorted. "Yes, exactly that. I can tell you how I want you to suck me and rim me. I can tell you how hard I am for you. I can describe exactly how I want to fuck that delicious ass."

I squirmed. "Not helping."

He cleared his throat. "Sorry. Okay, I'm going to try to get through this without sounding like a total idiot."

"Would it help if I said I think this thing between us moved to something more than just some random hookups and kinda slapped me in the face with the intensity of how much you started to mean to me? And then when we got smacked with the shared lease and pulled away from each other, I realized that I missed what we had. But we were both acting like fools and let it get in the way of any type of relationship. Would any of that help you get started?" My face burned hot as the words spilled and my heart sped up when Rhys took my hand.

"God, yes. That helps." He took a deep breath. "At first, I just didn't want to share. Then when I realized it meant we'd be creating our art in the same space, my insecurities took over. I worried you'd see that I'm not perfect, you'd see that my art isn't the best. I imagined these scenarios where crowds came to the shop and everyone was there to buy from you, but they only laughed at my work. I worried that you'd make so much more money because you were able and wanted to give lessons. I don't have that talent or desire." Rhys ran his thumb over my hand. "Then I got pissed because my creativity started to suffer and I blamed you. It wasn't until Caroline and Bode talked to us that I finally admitted to myself that my work was suffering because I missed you. I miss us."

"And how are you feeling about the studio and your work now?" I pulled my leg up to curl it under me and leaned into Rhys's side.

"I'm not sure I'll ever be one hundred percent confident in my work. But I loved what you said about bringing together our similarities and differences, both in *us* and in our work." Rhys leaned over to kiss me. "I'm sorry I acted like I thought you'd copy my work. That was an asshole thing to say. I know you'd never."

"So, what are you feeling about this?" I gestured between us.

"I want it. I want it back like it was, but...I know this may sound selfish, and maybe you aren't on the same page, I'd like it to be *more*." Rhys's eyes met mine.

"More? If by more you mean we date and do normal couple stuff along with the amazing sex, I'm so totally on that page." I nuzzled his neck. "I think what we started was fine when we thought it would be a few hookups and maybe some casual sex for a few months. But when we started to realize we had more of a connection, we weren't sure how to handle that. Then the building screw-up threw us for a loop for sure." I kissed along his jaw. "I think we're lucky we both have siblings to set us straight and tell us to get our heads out of our asses. I think the exact words Bode used were 'Suck it up, Buttercup.'"

Rhys chuckled. "Caroline basically said the same. Even my dead father got in on the fun. Today, all I could think of was a phrase he used to say. *You gotta risk it if you want the biscuit.* Those words are what finally gave me the courage to ask you to come over tonight."

"So, wait. Am I the biscuit?" I teased.

Rhys was quiet for a moment. "I think you're the biscuit on a small scale. On a larger scale, the biscuit is happiness, contentment, love, success."

My heart soared and I whispered, "You want to risk it?"

Rhys studied me for several beats before smiling. "I do. I want to risk it. I want to risk the feelings and emotions and possible heartache, and I want to do it with you. If you'll have me."

"I'll take that risk as long as you're by my side." I fought the sting of tears and swallowed the lump in my throat.

"Come on, my biscuit. I think we've done enough talking for now." Rhys stood from the couch and pulled me to stand with him. "You okay with that?"

I nodded. "I'm so okay with that." My body sang with anticipation. Sex with Rhys had been amazing since that first time and had gotten better every time since. I couldn't explain why it always seemed so fantastic. It was like we had this physical connection, but it went beyond that. And it made our recent struggle to communicate even more frustrating and confusing. How could two people be so drawn to each other, so in-tune to each other, so connected on a physical level, yet unable to express feelings and emotions? I guess we were more mature and intelligent in some ways than others. My heart was full; I had high hopes that this was a turning point for us.

* * *

"I want to do everything, all at once." Rhys stripped his

shirt over his head and shucked his pants and underwear off in one swift move.

I swallowed thickly as his dick slapped his lower abdomen. I yanked my shirt over my head and removed my pants. With my cock straining behind the orange mesh, I cupped myself. "Suck me." My breath hitched as Rhys hooked his thumbs in the waistband of my underwear.

"Did you wear these for me?" He kissed my neck, his lips and tongue hot against my skin.

I nodded.

Rhys shimmied the mesh down my legs.

I kicked and the orange material flew across the room.

"Lie down, head at the foot of the bed." Rhys gave me a tiny push.

When he joined me on the bed, with his head at the opposite end, I knew what he wanted and my mouth watered. I reached for his hips and pulled him close, nuzzled the light thatch of neatly trimmed hair at the base of his cock, and trailed my tongue along the throbbing vein until I reached his leaking slit. I tongued him and savored his salty bitterness. As I played and teased, Rhys gripped my cock and stroked before sucking me deep to the back of his throat.

I gasped and thrust deep. "You want me to fuck your face?"

Rhys nodded as his hot, wet mouth devoured my cock.

"Only if you do the same. I want to choke on this beautiful dick." I gripped Rhys's ass and pulled him forward so his hard length slid deep in my mouth.

We thrust and sucked, swallowed and gagged, fondled each other's balls and teased fingers at the other's pucker.

My balls drew up tight as Rhys's finger slipped deeper into my hole. My release shot deep in his throat and I shuddered as he took all of what I gave him. Knowing I wanted to do more to Rhys, I popped off his cock before he could come.

Rhys groaned in protest, but I rolled him to his stomach and lifted his hips. As his legs spread and his gorgeous ass opened for me, I licked my lips. Pressing kisses along the round globes of his ass, I trailed a finger against his hole. I placed hands on both cheeks and exposed his dusky pink pucker. I blew against his sensitive skin before flicking my tongue into the most intimate part of his body.

Rhys moaned. "Enjoy my ass while you can, because next round I'm going to own your hole."

"Promises, promises," I murmured before dipping my tongue into his tightness. I buried my face deep and breathed in the fresh scent of soap and Rhys's familiar musk. "Stroke yourself," I commanded.

Rhys reached for his cock and I took his fist in mine and pumped.

"I'm gonna come, Benji. Fuck me with your tongue." Rhys panted and thrust into our joined hands.

I pressed my tongue against his hole and thrust in and out until his body tensed and he spilled himself with a roar.

Rhys collapsed and I moved to lie next to him. "Rest up," he murmured.

"Cuddle with me for twenty minutes. I'll be good to go by then." I allowed Rhys to wrap his arms around me and I snuggled into his chest. Being back in Rhys's embrace felt like everything was right in the world.

10

RHYS

BENJI WAS BACK in my arms, in my bed, in my life and it felt as if all was right in the world. How could one person complete me so completely? We had to work on our communication, especially when it came to our artwork and the business and things we were somewhat unpracticed at and insecure with. But sex with Benji, holding him in my arms, was like the perfect puzzle piece clicking into place. Like my heart, body, and mind all sighed and everything aligned just right. All because of this man.

We dozed for a bit.

I woke him with nibbles on his earlobe. "You want to eat?"

"Mmm," he mumbled. "Still full from eating your ass," he teased.

I snorted. "In that case, I'm gonna fuck you until you're trembling and begging. Then I'll let you come. We can eat cold pizza later." I pressed my thickening cock against him. "Will you stay the night?" Was that too much? Was I moving too quickly?

"I packed a bag. Left it in the car, just in case you didn't want me to."

"I want you to," I mumbled against his mouth before I kissed him.

"And I want you to fuck me." Benji rolled from my arms and rummaged in the bedside table. He produced a condom and lube with a smile, but his face fell into a frown.

"What's wrong?" I took his hand.

"Just a thought that maybe the condoms and lube in that drawer weren't there just for us. Were you with anyone after me?" He worried his bottom lip. "Not that it's a deal-breaker. I know we hadn't agreed to anything exclusive."

I shook my head. "No. No one else. Not while I was with you and not since you. I was too busy with the studio. And I didn't want anyone else."

He smiled softly and nodded. "Same." He tossed the foil packet and bottle to the side. "I think you promised to fuck me." Benji moved to the middle of the bed and got on all fours, ass in the air, leaning on his elbows.

My dick moved from thick and heavy to hard and throbbing at the sight of Benji presenting himself for me to fuck, to take, to own. I moved behind him and tongued his ass until he was sloppy wet with my spit. I smacked my cock against his hole. When I should have reached for the condom and lube, I froze.

Benji glanced over his shoulder and wiggled his ass. "What's wrong?"

"I don't want to do it like this, roll over." I wasn't sure why, but our usual doggy style position seemed impersonal and cold. Like it was perfect for sex with a stranger, just right for random hook ups, exactly what I might have wanted with a casual partner. But it wasn't what I wanted with Benji.

Benji rolled over, his brows raised. "Better?" He spread his legs and stroked his hard length.

I nodded. "I'm not saying I won't fuck you that way ever again, but something about tonight seems more intimate. I want to see your face, want you to see my cock driving into your ass. Want to be able to kiss you." I reached for the foil packet, ripped it open and rolled the latex down my shaft. After a few pumps of lube, I slicked my cock and worked the liquid into Benji's ass. Pushing his knees toward his chest, I gripped my cock and pressed at his hole. I'd never tire of watching his body open for me, suck me in, cling to my dick. As I fed my length into him inch by inch, Benji gasped and held his legs behind his knees.

"Always feels like you're going to tear me open, so damn huge," Benji panted as he lifted his head to watch me take his ass.

"God, I've missed this. Missed your tight ass, missed holding you, touching you." I pressed the rest of the way in and groaned when my balls pressed tightly against Benji's ass. "Missed you, *us*."

Benji whimpered. "I missed us too." He let his calves rest against my shoulders and gripped his cock in a fist. "Need you to fuck me now. Please."

I pulled out and slammed back in, reveling in the tight heat of Benji's body. I set a long, slow, hard thrusting rhythm and leaned forward to kiss him. "I never want to lose this again," I murmured against his lips.

"Same." Benji opened his mouth, our tongues thrusting together.

I'd missed everything about him. His touch, his kiss, his scent, his flavor. I wanted to keep him, protect him, own him. But as much as I wanted all that, I wanted to be his, let him protect me, be owned by him. The balance of strength and fragility between us heated my blood and made my heart thump harder. We were the same, yet different. Strong and independent, yet soft and needy. And I wanted it all, wanted it with Benji. With a groan, I rocked my cock hard and deep into his ass until he cried out and painted his stomach and chest. I thrust a few more times and unloaded deep in his hot channel.

After a few moments of catching my breath, I pulled out slowly.

Benji shifted his legs from their bent position with a moan. "Ahhh, gonna feel that tomorrow. I don't think my legs have ever bent that way."

I fell onto him and loved the way he twisted his legs up with mine. "That was fucking amazing." I kissed him. "You're amazing."

"We've got spunk drying between us. We should shower," Benji murmured against my neck. His stomach rumbled loudly.

We laughed.

"And then we should eat. I think my appetite is finally back."

Our steamy shower was unhurried as we lazily kissed and slowly stroked each other to gentle, shuddering orgasms.

"I hate that we lost any time, but I'm so glad we've found our way back to each other." I pressed Benji against the tile wall and licked water droplets from his jaw before teasing his lips with my tongue.

He cocked his head as if thinking. "I don't know. I agree that I hate we lost that time, but I honestly think it was good for us. As much as it sucked to find out about the building mess-up, sharing our studio likely allowed for us to stay together more so than separate businesses would have. I think we would have gone our separate ways and never come back together because of the competition factor. This way, we were forced to stay in close proximity and when we realized how much we missed each other, we didn't have such a vast distance separating us." He frowned. "Does that make sense? It sounded better in my head."

I kissed him hard, smacking our lips together. "It makes complete sense. I guess this is one of those situations where things going against our plans ended up working out better than we ever could have imagined."

"Yeah." Benji leaned his forehead against mine. "I'm excited to have you as my business partner and travel on this journey with you."

"So just business partners?" My gut twisted.

Benji smiled. "Business partners on this business journey. Friends and lovers on a personal journey?"

I thought about that for a moment. "Can we be all of the above on both journeys? Combine them all? Partners in business and on a personal side? Taking the whole journey together?"

Benji nodded. "Can't say I'm not a little scared of what

happens if the business or personal side of things take a turn for the worse."

"Let's not borrow trouble." I kissed his nose. "So, officially boyfriends? No more just random hooking up?"

"Oh, there will be random hooking up," Benji teased. "But I love the sound of boyfriends."

We dried off and I ran down to Benji's car for his bag.

When I returned, he was lounging naked on the couch.

"Mmm, maybe I should just keep you naked all the time." I tossed him his bag with a laugh.

.

* * *

We settled in with pizza, beers, and a movie. Within forty-five minutes, we realized we'd been talking and had no clue what the movie was about.

Benji yawned.

"You want to head to bed?" I turned off the television.

He nodded. "I need to set an alarm. I have to run home tomorrow to change before the studio opens."

I pulled him to his feet. "No worries. You think tomorrow will be as good as today was?"

Benji pursed his lips. "Actually, I'm thinking it could maybe be better. A lot of people will be off work, so I'm hoping we'll have a bigger crowd. Maybe some from today will come back?" He wrapped his arms around my neck and pulled me in for a kiss.

When I pulled away, I couldn't help but smile. "That would be amazing. Let's plan on tomorrow being as good or better than today. We'll need to get extra pastries in case we have a bigger crowd. Maybe some who visited today will be back to buy tomorrow."

We brushed our teeth, side-by-side at the sink, bumping hips and sharing frothy smiles, and I knew without a doubt that I'd never been so happy. My life seemed to be falling into perfect place and I couldn't help but think it was because I had Benji by my side.

I climbed into bed and let Benji be the big spoon. He pulled me close, our shirtless skin warm together, my ass fitting perfectly against his groin. His sharp intake of breath had me breathing heavily.

"We should sleep." I whispered and wiggled my ass against his plump cock.

"Yeah, we should. Which means you should probably stop rubbing your ass against me like that." Benji's soft, gravely words against my ear made me shiver.

"Or what?"

"Or I might get the wrong idea. Might think you're more interested in fucking than in sleeping." He reached down to stroke my cock.

"I want you in me." I pressed my dick against his palm and rubbed my ass against his now rock-hard cock.

Benji groaned. "Yes," he hissed. "Just like this. Take your pants off." He rolled to the side and I heard him rummaging for a condom.

I shucked my pants off and squeezed my shaft. I felt Benji take off his pants and heard the crinkle of the condom wrapper before the click of the lube bottle and then he was back against me.

"Lift this leg." He tapped my left leg.

I lifted my leg and draped it over his as his slick dick pressed against my ass.

Benji ran a slippery finger against my hole and teased into my body.

"Just want your cock," I pleaded.

Benji pressed his cock head at my pucker. "Don't want to hurt you."

"I like the sting." It was true. I was the one most often fucking Benji, but I enjoyed taking his long dick from time to time. And the stretch and sting were part of what I loved the most about it.

Benji moaned and slowly pushed into my ass. "Tell me if it's too much."

I gasped as my body fought against his invasion. Pushing back against him, I breathed through the hot pain. Then he slid inside and I sighed at how perfectly he fit in me.

"Fuck, you're like fire and so damn tight." Benji rocked his hips and fucked me with a strong, slow rhythm. He reached down and cupped my balls, pressed against my taint, and then took my hard length in his fist and stroked. "I want to fuck you bare. Want to fill you and watch it leak from your hole."

My breath caught in my chest. "Yes, want that. Can we? Get to the clinic and make sure we're free of anything?"

"Definitely. Can't wait to have your bare cock buried deep, your hot seed exploding in me. I want it to drip from my ass and feel you press it back in with your dick." Benji continued pumping into me and stroking my cock.

"Love it when you talk dirty." My balls drew up tight and I spilled over Benji's fist only seconds before he thrust deep and his dick pulsed in my ass.

After a quick clean up, we curled up together under the comforter.

"Goodnight," I whispered.

"G'night," Benji mumbled.

Our studio was open, we'd had a great first-day crowd, my *boyfriend* was back in my bed. Life was good. I couldn't wait to get busy on new pieces in the studio.

* * *

I came awake slowly and smiled at the warm skin plastered to my side. Benji was a cuddler and waking to his naked body pressed to mine was something I'd missed terribly.

"I gotta piss, but I wouldn't mind a quickie before I leave," Benji murmured against my shoulder as he rocked his hips against my thigh.

"Can probably be arranged." I palmed myself and groaned as I watched Benji roll from bed and saunter his perfect ass to the bathroom. I heard the toilet flush and then the sink turn on.

"No fair, if you get to brush your teeth, I get to too!" I stumbled from bed and met him as he exited the bathroom. "Give me thirty seconds. I want you on your hands and knees when I get back. Want to see that gorgeous ass spread out for me." I kissed his neck and breathed in his minty scent.

Somehow, I managed to piss without painting the wall, brushed my teeth in record time, and rushed back to bed.

Benji's strong, leanly muscled body took up the middle of the bed, his ass in the air, long legs spread apart. He leaned forward on his elbows and turned his head to watch me approach. "Like what you see?"

I grunted as I yanked a condom from the drawer and made short work of rolling it on and slicking myself with lube. As I crawled onto the bed, I leaned down to press kisses along Benji's spine. When I reached the cleft of his ass, I moved behind him and positioned myself between his legs. I gripped his hips and slid my cock between his cheeks.

"Don't play around, fuck me." Benji gripped the sheets and pushed his ass back. "Want it."

"Spread yourself," I commanded.

Benji did as he was told and I groaned as his long fingers pulled his fleshy globes apart and bared his hole.

Pressing my throbbing cock against his pucker, I pushed in slowly.

Benji whimpered with each additional inch I gave him. "Want it hard, fuck me hard."

I pulled back and slammed back in as I gripped Benji's hips.

He shifted so his arms could hold onto the headboard and my thrusts slammed the wood against the wall. Between the bed, my grunts, and Benji's moans, I was glad my room had two outside walls in the corner of my apartment building. We were loud.

Benji's noises spurred me on and I thrust harder just to make him get louder.

Leaning forward, I wrapped my arms under Benji's armpits and around his chest. I pulled him upward and he turned his head for a hot, sloppy kiss.

I stopped pumping my hips while I kissed him and stroked his cock. "I want you flat on your stomach so I can fuck you into this mattress."

Benji whimpered his agreement and dropped to his stomach. He spread his legs and I loved that he was so into sex. Had he been as vocal and pliant and exuberant with other partners? I slid my cock into his ass; I didn't even want to think of Benji with other people.

I gripped his hands and thrust hard and fast into his tight hole. When I couldn't stay up on my arms any longer, I dropped on his back and maneuvered us slightly to our left sides.

Benji pulled his right leg up and reached for his cock.

"Yeah, fuck your fist. Come for me." I pumped hard and deep until Benji cried out and tensed in my arms.

"Fuuuuck," he roared.

I shuddered and blew my load deep in his ass. My cock pulsed over and over, Benji's tight hole milking every drop from me. "Gonna do that bare. Soon."

Benji shivered and gripped my hand. "Don't know why the idea of that turns me on so damn much, but I can't wait."

I pulled out, tossed the condom, and gathered a heavy, cuddly Benji close. My heart nearly burst with the barrage of emotions ping-ponging in my head and heart. I wanted to whisper *I love you*, but it was too soon. Right? We'd been having casual sex. *Great* casual sex, but still. Then we basically broke up because of the studio. And, just the day before, finally had our asses kicked into gear so that we could get back to where we'd been and *more*. Declarations of love may have been making it hard for me to breathe, but it was definitely too soon to admit them out loud.

Instead, I kissed the side of his head. "You're amazing. As much as I hate to say it, we better clean up so you can go home and get dressed. I'll get the pastries. I'm planning on staying after hours today to work in the studio."

Benji sighed. "Do you care if I do the same? I was hoping to throw some pottery."

"Mmmm, wet clay? Can you do it naked? We could always clean up upstairs." I was joking. Mostly. The idea of a naked tryst with Benji at his pottery wheel definitely held plenty of appeal.

He chuckled. "We'll see. Either way, I say we make use of that upstairs *soon*. Shame to let a perfectly good shower, bed, couch, and ugly chaise lounge go to waste."

"You going to tell your brother and the guys about us?" My heart stuttered with the unexpected thought that I *wanted* him to tell them about us. I wanted to be part of that portion of his life. If he'd have me.

Shit. Maybe I was getting too far ahead of myself. Maybe he wasn't ready for that.

"For sure."

I let loose a breath I hadn't realized I was holding.

"You want to meet them? Like officially where we have more time to hang? Maybe we could all go out? At least hang out casually even if not a full-blown group date."

I nodded. "Yeah, sounds good."

Benji rolled from the bed and wiped himself with a discarded t-shirt.

"Hey, that's my shirt." I yanked it away from him.

He laughed. "Well, we've definitely shared bodily fluids over the last twenty-four hours, I guess you'll just have to wash it along with your sheets."

I opened my arms and my entire body warmed as Benji smiled and walked into my embrace. We hugged for several beats before I cupped his face and kissed him, slow and deep. I broke the kiss and whispered, "I'm really glad we finally talked and figured our shit out."

Benji pulled away and gazed into my eyes. "Same." He nodded, smiled, and started to speak again, but clamped his mouth shut.

"What?" I frowned.

"Nothing. Just totally agree. So glad we talked and got over ourselves." He planted a final kiss on my mouth before dressing quickly. "I'll see you in about an hour?"

I nodded. I was sure he had started to say something else. But what? And why had he stopped? I shrugged internally, walked him to the door, and couldn't help the smile that filled my face for the next hour while I showered, dressed, and walked to the bakery.

I was walking on air and as giddy as a kid with their first love.

11

BENJI

HOLY SHIT.

I leaned my forehead against the wet tile as hot water streamed over me.

I'd nearly said *I love you* to Rhys.

Pretty sure I'd looked like a fool stopping and clamming up like I did. I shook my head. It was *way too soon*. How were the feelings so damn strong? Rhys and I had known each other for a bit, but surely my feelings were just the sex and infatuation talking, right?

As I shampooed my hair, I thought about my feelings for Rhys.

I liked spending time with him. For a brief time, that hadn't been the case, but now that we were back in a groove it was totally true. I enjoyed our conversations. I looked forward to when I'd see him again. I admired his artistic talents. I'd been a mess when we weren't seeing each other. I'd be sad if we broke up; I'd definitely miss him.

Were those indicators of love?

Physically, my heart beat faster and my skin heated when we were close. My body longed for his touch. Not just *any* touch, Rhys's touch. I was warm and safe and *home* in his embrace.

Yeah. I loved Rhys.

But no way I could spring that on him so soon.

I finished my shower and joined the guys in the living room.

"Ah, look at you. You're all aglow and shit." Bode nudged my knee with his foot from his place next to Sage on the loveseat as I sat in the recliner.

My face heated.

"Ohhh, is our little Benji *in love*?" Kyson placed a hand over his heart and swooned.

I couldn't stop the quick glance I made around the room.

Sage gasped. "Hey, guys? Maybe cut the teasing routine." He aimed a sympathetic gaze my way. "Do you love him? Rhys?"

Kyson and Bode's eyes grew wide. The two men who had known me from birth were stunned silent. They'd seen me through juvenile crushes, a few first loves, and several disappointing casual dating situations. But they'd never once seen me in a serious relationship—not for lack of trying—and most definitely never owning up to anything close to being in love.

I shrugged. "I think I do." I scowled. "No, I know I do. Love Rhys, I mean." I ran a hand over my face and attempted to hide the growing grin tugging at my mouth.

"Wow, that's amazing. Really wondered if I'd ever see the day." Kyson reached across the coffee table next to me and slapped a warm hand on my arm. "Good for you."

Bode pulled Sage close to his side and smiled. "So, does this mean we get to *officially* meet him?"

"We've talked about you all meeting—longer than what you met at the opening—but we have *not* discussed this turn of events regarding feelings. That topic is off the table when you meet him." I lost myself in thought for a moment as I stared at the landscape piece on the far wall. "I think I'm having trouble believing that I feel this way. I completely *do* feel it, but isn't it too soon? Too much?"

"I think when you *know*, you just know." Sage smiled lovingly at Bode. "How do you think Rhys feels?"

"I don't know. He seems really into our getting back together and dating, but I can't exactly be like, *Listen, I think I love you. But I don't want to say anything in case you don't love me back, so if you could just let me know how you're feeling, that would be great.*" I sighed.

"Just enjoy your time together. One or both of you will know when it's time to take the next step." Kyson shifted on his recliner and rocked slightly.

"What about you and Bay taking the next step?" I raised my brow. I was being pushy, I knew I was. But I knew Bay and Kyson liked each other and I imagined them being so great together. I wanted my cousin happy and in a loving, healthy relationship.

Kyson scoffed. "Next step? There's no next step for Bay and me. There is no Bay and me. I'm interested, but he's busy and trying to be a good parent to Arlo. I can't argue that without sounding like a complete ass. I'd never want to interfere with something as important as Arlo being loved and protected." He pursed his lips together and wrinkled his nose. "As much as we seem to like each other and mesh, the timing just isn't right."

"Gah, how can I argue that?" My brows drew together. "The sexual tension between you two is palpable and I think you'd be so great together. But you can't fight timing."

"Doesn't mean the timing will always be wrong." Bode smiled like a damn cat who ate a canary. "Sometimes you just have to catch up with the timing. You'll know when it's right."

Sage snorted. "He falls in love after fighting it for so long and now he's a damn relationship expert."

We all laughed.

"I'm going to the studio. Second day of the opening. Hoping for bigger and better than yesterday." I stood.

"Bro, yesterday was amazing. Be proud." Bode moved so that Sage could stretch his long legs out on the couch.

"I'm proud and really happy. Just looking forward to the same or better." I winked and slipped my shoes on. "See you if you stop by, if not then I'll see you for breakfast tomorrow." Our Sunday breakfast or brunch and grocery shopping was something we worked hard to keep sacred and protected. I wasn't against inviting Rhys, but I wasn't going to cancel with the guys because of Rhys.

As I walked down the stairs, I thought about that. Rhys meant something to me. Rhys meant *a lot* to me. The fact that I was interested in bringing him *into* my family and friendship instead of skipping out on the guys was something new indeed. And maybe part of the reason these feelings were so different and overwhelming.

* * *

By the time day two of the grand opening wrapped up, I

was grinning from ear to ear and couldn't wait to replay it all with Rhys once we closed.

He was at the sales counter ringing up *five* final purchases. Our sales had been spectacular all day.

I winked at him before making my way over to a particular customer I'd been hoping to speak to before he left. Bay and his mom had brought Arlo in about thirty minutes earlier. I didn't think I was going to get a chance to speak to him, but as luck would have it, Bay's mother recognized Rhys's sister, Caroline. The two women had been sipping tea and chatting with no signs of stopping while Bay and Arlo enjoyed the artwork, pastries, and the little children's paint area I'd set up.

I approached Bay as he smiled at Arlo painting a picture on a little easel. "Thanks for coming in, Bay." I shook his hand when he turned my way.

"Not a problem. Arlo loved everything he saw and he *definitely* wants to take lessons. Let me know when you start those and what you think would be best for him to begin with."

"For sure. I'd love to have him as a student." I wasn't completely sure, but I had a feeling that Bay struggled here and there trying to stretch money to cover Arlo's needs and wants. The little boy was well taken care of, for sure. I just wondered how much of a strain it was on Bay's finances to become a parent with very little time to prepare. I'd be sure to price Arlo's lessons *very* affordably. I pushed the thought from my mind and waited a beat before dipping my toe in the water so to speak. "Looks like you're settling into parenting like a total pro. Arlo seems to be doing so great with you."

Bay huffed but smiled. "Hardest job I've ever done.

Exhausting both mentally and physically. Scary as shit. And so frustrating. I feel like I never know what I'm doing or what's going to happen. And if I have a plan, I can pretty much only count on nothing to go as planned." He shook his head and continued to smile. "But there's nothing better than being his dad. Nothing harder, scarier, or more exhausting, but nothing better."

I smiled as my gut fluttered a bit. Children weren't something I'd ever thought about, didn't even know if I'd ever want to be a parent. But Bay hadn't planned on becoming a father basically overnight, and here he was doing a damn great job of it. Didn't sound easy, but I could appreciate how rewarding of a job it was for him.

"So, this is maybe a bit forward of me." I grimaced. "Okay, it's *a lot* forward of me."

Bay smiled and raised his brows expectantly.

"I get the feeling you and Kyson could be amazing together. I know there's definitely attraction there." I didn't let him interrupt, just barreled on. "Sage, Bode, and I *love* watching Arlo and you know we do a good job of it. I'd like to offer our babysitting services—either Sage and Bode or Rhys and me or all four of us—so you and Kyson could go out on a real date. Would hate to see nothing happen between you guys just because you never gave it a chance."

Bay took a deep breath and blew it out slowly. "My gut response is to say no because I need to focus on Arlo. But my mom recently jumped my ass about using Arlo as an excuse to not date."

I smiled hopefully.

Bay held up a hand. "I'm not agreeing to anything. But I'm not saying no. If I decide to ask Kyson out, I'd be completely comfortable with you and Rhys or Sage and Bode watching Arlo."

When I did a silly little fist pump, we both laughed.

"Speaking of you and Rhys. Is that a *thing* now? I'd heard things got a little messed up and dramatic for a bit."

Rhys sidled up at that moment and took my hand. "Mistakes were made, drama ensued, but we're back on the right track for now."

Bay smiled at our joined hands.

Did I imagine the wistful look on his face?

Arlo finished his painting just as Bay was saying, "Well, that's great to hear."

I helped Arlo clean up his paint station and showed him the paint racks where his picture could dry. "You and Daddy can come in and pick it up in a day or so."

Caroline and Ms. Whitfield finished their tea and pastries.

Within ten minutes, the studio was empty, the doors locked, and the lights off.

"I think we agreed to some studio time with possible sexy encounters?" Rhys waggled his brows.

"I'm sure it can be arranged." I pulled him close and kissed him deeply before pulling back. "Hi. I feel like we didn't get to chat much today."

Rhys explored my mouth, his tongue mating with mine.

When we broke apart, panting, he smiled. "Super busy with customers and sales is a great reason to have no time to chat."

"I say we put on our music and work for ninety minutes. After that, anything goes." I nibbled along his jaw.

"Perfect plan. I'm going to change into some work clothes. I'll see you in ninety." Rhys gave me a final kiss and headed up the stairs to change clothes.

I cleaned up the pastries, the coffee and tea station, and the children's paint area. After dusting the displays, I went upstairs. Glad that I'd thought ahead to leave work clothes at the studio, I changed into a t-shirt and jeans that I didn't mind getting messy.

Popping in earbuds, I found the music I wanted and hit play before immersing myself in painting and glazing a few pottery pieces. Soon, I moved to finalizing some jewelry pieces and adding finishing touches to an abstract landscape painting I was stoked to put up for sale. Finally, when all the bits and pieces of finishing were complete, I set to work with my clay and wheel.

I loved all of my art mediums, fell hard for different pieces for different reasons, lost myself in various projects depending on what I was feeling at the moment. But working with a clump of raw clay on my wheel was something that never failed to bring me peace and comfort. With music blaring in my head, I slapped the two-pound ball of clay onto the wheel and began the work of centering it and expressing the air bubbles. Within minutes, I was deep into my work.

I spent the next hour manipulating the cool, damp clay. When the piece was exactly the way I imagined it, I stopped the wheel and transferred the vase to dry. I'd work with it again when it was ready for the next steps.

A hand on my shoulder caused me to jump, but I settled immediately when I realized it was Rhys. I took out my earbuds.

"Will you teach me how to do that?" Rhys pointed toward the wheel.

"Of course." I nodded. "It's so relaxing."

"I've always been mesmerized watching it. But *you* make it particularly sensual."

I laughed. "I didn't even know you were watching, I was lost in my hands and the clay." I grabbed a new ball of clay and pointed to the stool. "Sit there. I'll sit behind you."

Rhys took his seat and I pulled a second stool behind him.

"Oh my God, this is so Ghost-y." Rhys laughed.

"I think I was like five when that movie came out. I didn't see it until years later. It's good even if a little cheesy. Whoopie Goldberg makes the whole thing. She's great." I nestled against Rhys and put the lump of clay in his hand.

"It's colder and heavier than I was expecting." Rhys tested the feel and weight of the clay in his hand.

"Yeah, people are usually surprised at the chill." I held his right hand in mine. "You're going to throw the clay down hard. It needs to splat and kinda flatten."

Rhys did as I instructed. The clay slapped against the wheel with a satisfying thud.

"Nice. Okay, I'm going to run the wheel. I'll guide your hands. We can make a bowl if you want, or just learn the feel of the clay." My whole body warmed where we touched. His hips and ass pressed into my spread legs, my arms wrapped around him, our skin touching. I nuzzled against his ear and kissed along his jaw.

"You keep doing that and I'll lose interest in the clay

very quickly." Rhys allowed me to move his hands along the clay as the wheel whirred to life.

I spent several moments showing Rhys what different finger and hand positions would make the clay do, how a different pressure would cause the clay to react in a completely different way.

"This is so amazing and beautiful. So satisfying to watch." Rhys turned his head to look over his shoulder while I held his hands in mine and shaped the clay. "I want your clothes off," he whispered the gruff words just barely loud enough for me to hear over the wheel.

"Then it's only fair if yours are off too." I stopped the wheel and reached for a wet towel to wipe our hands.

Within seconds, we'd stripped to our underwear and returned to our places on the stools. I wrapped my arms around Rhys's body and took his hands in mine again as my thighs pressed against his hips and legs. Dribbling water from a sponge, I showed Rhys how the addition of water would change the way the clay responded to his touch.

Slowly, I removed my hands from Rhys's and allowed him to manipulate the clay on his own. My fingers trailed along his legs and inner thighs before teasing his growing bulge. I traced the light path of hair from the waistband of Rhys's underwear up to where it spread between his pecs. I knew I was leaving a mess of wet clay water as my hands roamed his body, but I didn't care. As I caressed both nipples and squeezed Rhys's chest in my hands, he dropped his hands from the clay and put his hands on my legs. I stopped applying pressure to the pedal and the wheel slowed to an eventual stop. My arms tightened around Rhys's chest and my now-hard cock pressed against his lower back as he squeezed my thighs with clay damp hands. Rhys's head fell back on my shoulder and I devoured his neck with hot, wet kisses as I teased his nipples with my nails.

"As much as I love learning to work with clay, my mind has suddenly gone elsewhere. Upstairs?" Rhys turned his head and kissed me.

I nodded and stood. "Toss that clay in the bucket and put the lid on tight." I grabbed the wet towel. When Rhys turned away from storing the clay, I brushed the cloth against his nipples.

He hissed.

"Sorry, but I plan to lick and bite these, clay doesn't taste great." I roughed his nipples until they were nearly clay-free. "Grab your clothes. We can wash a load of laundry while we're otherwise occupied."

We grabbed our clothes and rushed up the stairs.

I stripped out of my underwear and socks and tossed all my clothes in the washing machine. Rhys did the same. We soaped and scrubbed our hands at the kitchen sink to remove most of the clay residue. When our hands were dry, Rhys pressed me against the counter and kissed me as our hard cocks rubbed together.

"Want to fuck you," Rhys murmured into my mouth.

"Well, it's your lucky day, because I want you to fuck me as well." I bit his lip and took his fine ass in my hands. "Go lay on the ugly ass chaise lounge. We'll christen it and put the damn eye sore to good use."

I rummaged in the bathroom until I found the lube and condoms Rhys had stocked. The sight of Rhys stretched out on the chaise lounge while he stroked his cock was almost too much.

I tossed the supplies on the small end table before straddling his waist and leaning down to capture his mouth. Shifting lower, I teased and nibbled at his nipples, smiling as they puckered into hard, red nubs. I sat astride Rhys's hips and rutted our dicks together, stroking them in my fist, and thumbing his leaking slit.

When I couldn't take it any longer, I tore open the condom wrapper, rolled the sheath onto him, and spread lube up and down his shaft before applying a few generous pumps to my fingers and smearing it around and into my hole. Tossing the lube to the side, I sat atop Rhys and reached behind me to grip his cock. I positioned his head at my slick pucker and pressed down. Rhys held still and moaned as I sank lower and lower on his throbbing length. Once I'd bottomed out, I raised and lowered myself a couple times, reveling in the heady power trip of controlling him even as his cock was buried in my ass. I leaned forward, gripping the back of the chaise lounge, and started a slow rhythm of fucking myself on Rhys's thick length.

"Fuck me," I whispered.

My position allowed me to straddle him, spread my knees, and hold myself up against the head of the lounge while watching his face. Rhys stared at me as he began to pump hard and slow into my ass. The rhythm soon changed to hard and fast as Rhys pummeled my hole with strong thrusts I felt throughout my entire body. He gripped my hips to hold me in one place as he set a punishing pace.

When he took my throbbing cock in his fist and began to pump, I lost all semblance of control and exploded long, thick ropes across his abdomen and chest.

"Yes, come for me." Rhys ran his fingers through the splatters and spread the jizz along my bottom lip before pulling me down to lick the smear from my lips and kiss me deeply. He held me tight against him and thrust hard and deep a few more times before groaning and pulsing his load into my ass.

By the time we'd both caught our breath and come down from our mutual highs, the washer was done. I tossed the clothes into the dryer. "Shower?"

Our shower was slow and sensual. I fingered Rhys's ass, playing with his prostate while kissing him and talking dirty, until he came with a silent shudder. Rhys dropped to his knees and sucked me, playing with my ass, teasing my sensitive hole with a wet finger, until I fisted his hair and spilled deep in his throat.

We lazily ended our shower, dried off, dressed in our original clothes and cuddled on the couch while the dryer finished its cycle.

"You want to come over and meet the guys properly? Maybe next weekend?" I figured Rhys could come after brunch and groceries. If the meeting went well, maybe he could do brunch and groceries with us the following weekend.

"I'd love to. I know I already know them somewhat, but it would be nice to officially meet them and hang out for a while." Rhys held my hand and kissed me. "I've *never* wanted to meet any friends or family, so this is all new to me."

My heart soared. "Kinda new to me as well. We'll take it one step at a time, yeah?"

"You want to go out on a real date before next

weekend?" Rhys's words were quiet and hesitant. "Drinks and food? Something casual?"

"We could meet at The Salty Lizard on Thursday night?" I swallowed thickly. "I told Bode I'd help cover an open shift, but as long as it's not super busy, I should be able to hang out. The food is good, Sage is a master mixologist, great atmosphere."

Rhys nodded as the dryer buzzed. "Sounds great."

We stored our work clothes for the next time they were needed, locked up the studio, shared a long, lingering kiss outside of the backdoor, and said good night. Tomorrow was our final day of the grand opening and nothing could erase the smile on my face.

Or the love in my heart.

But Rhys didn't need to know about that just yet.

12

RHYS

THURSDAY FOUND me dressed in a mint green button up, light wash jeans, and a worn pair of chucks. I topped the look with a brown leather bomber jacket and aviator sunglasses. I appreciated the vibrant colors of The Salty Lizard's logo as I pulled open the door and walked in. A momentary zing of apprehension immediately dissipated when I saw Benji drop a towel and approach with a huge smile.

"Hey," he whispered and kissed my cheek. He pulled back. "Sorry, was that okay?"

I nodded. The bar was full, but the atmosphere was one of welcome acceptance and camaraderie. I kissed Benji's full lips. "It's perfect."

Benji smiled, took my hand, and led me to a corner table. "Our finest table for you, sir." He pulled a chair out for me. "I'm going to let Bode know you're here and put some food in for us. What do you want to drink? I'll get Sage busy on it." Benji poured two glasses of water and placed a bowl of chips in front of me.

"Tell him to surprise me with something he loves to make." I popped a chip in my mouth.

"Sounds good. I think the guys can cover me for a while, so once the food's ready, I'll be all yours." He leaned down and kissed me. "Maybe tonight we can end up in my bed or yours?"

I groaned. "Definitely. Now go so you can get back here. I want my full date experience." I smacked his ass.

Benji laughed and sauntered away.

Within fifteen minutes, Benji and Bode approached the table with food and drinks.

"Sage says this is his famous Purple People Eater." Benji placed a large round glass in front of me.

A gorgeous purple liquid filled the glass and a sparkly purple sugar decorated the rim.

"It's beautiful. Almost too pretty to drink." I took a sip. "But it's delicious so I'll drink it no matter how pretty it is."

Bode held out a hand. "Good to see you again. I know we know each other, but figure we can make it official. I'm Bode."

I chuckled and shook his hand. "Rhys. Nice to meet you."

Bode sat with us.

"I promise he's not crashing our date." Benji nudged his twin.

"Nah, just thought we could shoot the shit for a bit." Bode leaned back in his chair.

Benji narrowed his eyes. "What's up?"

"Porn Brothers are coming to visit." Bode crossed his arms over his chest.

Benji groaned. "Noooo. For what?"

I raised my hand. "Um, excuse me? The Porn Brothers?" I was confused and intrigued.

Benji rolled his eyes. "Our dad and uncle. Their names are Dick Silver and Rod Silver which we've always thought sounded like terrible porn names."

"Wow." I took a drink and savored the sweet and sour liquid. "Yeah, those are bad. Do Dick and Rod have a sense of humor about it?"

"Eh, Rod is Kyson's dad. He's *kinda* okay with it. He's less of an asshole than Dick. But Rod has his issues as well." Benji dipped a tater tot in ketchup and popped it in his mouth.

"Dick Silver is exactly as his name would have you believe. A complete and total dick." Bode scowled. "You should hope and pray you never have to meet him, but if you're going to be part of our family you likely won't get so lucky."

"Don't scare him." Benji elbowed Bode and looked at me. "Our dad is as self-absorbed, materialistic, and unwaveringly and dominatingly judgmental as a person can be."

A queasy feeling began in my stomach. "So, he's homophobic?"

"Actually, our sexuality is one of his least complaints. He doesn't love it, but he doesn't really ride us for that." Benji gave his brother a look. "Dick has always been hardest on Bode."

"Why?" I didn't like Dick Silver already.

"Because I struggled in school. I drew attention to the Silver name by not being perfect. I was loud and active. I think the only reason Dick doesn't get too riled up about us being gay is because he can use it to his benefit. *Look at me. I'm an open and accepting father and uncle.* When in reality he doesn't give two shits. He uses his money and status in our small town to hold power over people." Bode rocked in his chair. "He *invested* money in The Salty Lizard and then used it to manipulate and threaten me. Would come up here and make comments about how he didn't like the way I was putting his investment to use and threaten to pull his financial support."

My eyes grew wide. I was young when my parents died, but I couldn't imagine having a father who would treat his child like that. "But The Salty Lizard seems to be doing great. What could he have possibly had to complain about?"

"The Lizard *is* doing great which is likely what rankled him. But he'd never admit that. So, I got a loan and bought him out. He has no control over my place anymore." Bode smirked.

"So why are the brothers coming here?" Benji asked as he wiped his hands on a napkin.

Bode shrugged. "Guess they have a training seminar up here. Rod told Kyson they were going to eat at the Lizard and stop by the studio." He laughed. "I think Kyson was worried they'd ask for massages."

"Ewww, can you imagine having to rub down either of those two?" Benji wrinkled his nose. "Our dad and uncle have not aged well."

"Probably all the drinking and lavish lunches." Bode stole an onion ring. "At least they'll see that all three of us are doing great and our businesses are thriving." He looked toward the bar. "I gotta get back to work. Take as long as you want. We've got it covered up there." He turned to me. "See you Sunday?"

I nodded.

When he was gone, Benji moved closer to me. "Sorr
about that, didn't mean to air our dirty laundry. I could
tell Bo was worried about something so I had to ask."

"Not a problem." I said the words, but apprehension
was building in my gut.

We finished the food and drinks. Benji brought two
more drinks to the table and grimaced. "Hey, I need to
cover Bode while he stocks the liquor. Shouldn't take
more than ten or fifteen minutes."

I nodded and took a drink. The alcohol warmed me
nicely.

"Seat taken?" A gentleman I recognized gestured to
the chair. He was likely ten years older than me and wore
the silver fox look very well. Whitfield? His mother and
Caroline knew each other. *Bay*. Bay Whitfield. The guy
Benji thought Kyson should be with.

I shook my head. "Please." I pushed out the chair with
my foot.

"Bay Whitfield. I think we know each other but not
officially." He held out his hand.

"Rhys Golden. Nice to meet you." I glanced around.
"Where's your little boy?"

"Mom is watching him while I grab food. He loves the
pretzel bites from here, but I don't bring him in when it's
busy. If they aren't packed, I can bring him in and Bode
will let him sit at the bar and eat pretzel bites and
chocolate milk." Bay gestured over his shoulder. "Bode
used to hate me. Thought I had something for Sage. But
he's always been amazing with Arlo."

I smiled. "Yeah, all the guys seem good with him." I
frowned.

"What's wrong?" Bay sipped a glass of water he'd been holding when he approached my table.

"Do you know the guys' dads? Dick and Rod?"

Bay snorted. "The Porn Brothers?"

I nodded.

"Well, I know they're assholes. Dick more so than Rod. And Bode seems to get the brunt of Dick's judgment. But I've not met them in person." He took another drink. "Why?"

The alcohol loosened my tongue just enough that I was feeling chatty. "Well, I really like Benji. He's great. We're officially dating and things are good."

Bay raised his brows. "But?"

I leaned forward on my elbows as if I had a secret to tell. "I can't deal with a crazy family. Crazy and drama ruin too many perfect relationships. I think I'm falling for Benji, but I don't want to get involved with someone who brings a ton of family baggage."

Bay pursed his lips. "First, if you think your relationship is perfect or expect it to be, you better check that shit quickly. No relationship is perfect."

I eyed him over the glass as I slurped down the purple goodness.

"Second, no family is perfect. Ever. In the history of families, there's never been an *actually* perfect family. Even if they *appear* perfect, they aren't. You know that saying? *Every family has that one person.* There's always a person or people who bring their own flavor of crazy to the family. It's what makes families what they are."

I shook my head. "Nope. I don't buy it. My sister is amazing. Her late husband was great. Her kids are successful, good people. My parents were beyond fantastic. We didn't do drama then and we don't do drama now. My family is proof that families *can* be perfect."

Bay smirked. "You ever heard the rest of that saying?"

I frowned and waited.

"Every family has that one person. If you think your family doesn't, then you're probably that one person." Bay raised his brow and watched me over his glass as he drained his water. "I'm just sayin' that no one is perfect, no family is perfect, and no relationship is perfect. Don't run from something that could be amazing just because you're scared of imperfection. *Perfection* doesn't exist." He turned toward the bar when his name was called. "That's my order, gotta go. Don't lose something because it's not perfect."

I started to speak, to protest, but I snapped my mouth shut and just waved him on his way. *Shit.* Was Bay right? I wanted to be offended; I *was* slightly offended. But was I the person in my family that wasn't perfect? Did I bring drama and craziness?

"Rhys, you've got to stop worshipping the distorted memories you have of Mom and Dad. They were far from perfect." The words Caroline had spoken to me time and time again echoed in my head. *"Mom and Dad had arguments, they had fights. They disagreed. They yelled. There was never abuse, but they weren't always sunshine and roses. My own marriage was far from perfect. Stan could be a complete ass, God rest his soul. And I can be a nightmare."*

I chuckled. I definitely agreed that Caroline could be a handful.

Did Mom and Dad really fight? I remembered them only as happy and loving parents. Was Caroline right? Had I formed these perfect memories of them in my grief?

Maybe.

But did I want to get in a relationship with Benji when it was evident he had a shitty father and drama abounded?

"Hey, what's up?" Benji sat next to me and put his hand on my thigh. "You look a million miles away."

I drained the rest of my drink for a bit of liquid courage. "My usual reaction would be to clam up, ignore the issue, and let it fester until I blow up."

"Issue? What issue?" Benji scowled and he took my hand. "What's wrong?"

I took a deep breath. "But I know we have to talk about things. Not talking about things is how we almost lost each other."

"Rhys, you're scaring me. What's going on?" He glanced around as if trying to figure out what had brought on my behavior.

"I love that drink. I wish I had another one. But it's strong and my teeth are already tingling, so I'll stop before I can't get the words out." I chugged an entire glass of water knowing I needed to hydrate after the sweet alcoholic concoction. "I have this thing with *perfect*. Perfect families, perfect relationships, perfect art, perfect people."

Benji cocked his head to the side but stayed quiet and let me talk.

"Until recently, I remembered my parents' marriage as perfect. Remembered them as perfect. Thought of my family as perfect." I ran a hand over my face. "Imperfection, drama, craziness scares me. It makes me nervous. It makes me run."

"Okay," Benji drew out the word. "I'm far from perfect. Is that what this is about?"

"The Porn Brothers freak me the fuck out. They sound crazy and dramatic and I'm scared of what type of trouble and chaos they could cause." The words rushed from me in one long whoosh.

Benji's brows raised and he broke into a smile. "The Porn Brothers *are* crazy and dramatic and they do cause trouble and chaos." He squeezed my hand. "But Bode, Kyson, and I are nothing like them and we're grownups who have chosen to keep Dick and Rod in our lives but at a distance. And our mothers are amazing. The Silver family is so far from perfect, we likely couldn't even find it with a map." He chuckled. "But Bode, Kyson, and I have found a perfect imperfection with each other. Bode and Sage have their imperfectly perfect love. I'm hopeful Kyson and Bay may eventually work out something along the lines of perfect imperfection." Benji leaned close and nuzzled my ear as he whispered, "I'm not perfect. You're not perfect—I know you don't like to hear it, but it's true." He smiled against my cheek when I snorted. "Our art isn't perfect; our studio isn't perfect. Nothing is perfect. But I'm pretty sure I want to spend a very long time being imperfect with you."

My breath caught and my eyes stung. "I'm sorry. I'm learning something about myself lately and it's kinda hard to take in. I'm a bit self-absorbed it seems."

This time, Benji snorted and I couldn't help but laugh with him.

"And I'm having to reimagine what I always thought a perfect relationship would look like." I sighed. "Without *perfect*, it's just a relationship and I don't know what to make of that."

Benji held my hand and tipped up my chin.

"Nothing is *just* a relationship. Even without the *perfect*, it's *ours*. What we have, what we're building, what we may have down the road? It's all ours in its perfect imperfection and I wouldn't have it any other way." His lips feathered against mine as a hot tear fell down my cheek. "I want to learn about all of our imperfections with you by my side."

I took a shaky breath. "I want that too. Just be patient with me as I adjust my ideas on perfect, okay?"

"I know we have to talk about things. Not talking about things is how we almost lost each other." Benji repeated my earlier words and bit his lip.

"Now you're the one scaring me. What's up?"

"I know this is quick and maybe you don't feel the same." He took a deep breath. "But in the spirit of being perfectly imperfect, I have to tell you something even if the timing is all wrong."

My heart nearly thumped out of my chest. Anxious anticipation made it hard to breathe. I swallowed thickly and nodded.

"Rhys, I love you." Benji squeezed my hand.

A warmth spread through my chest and threatened to drown me. "Quite possibly the most perfect words I've ever heard." I kissed him. "I love you, too."

Benji grabbed my hand and we gave quick waves to Bode and Sage as we rushed out of The Salty Lizard.

We all but ran the few blocks to my apartment.

* * *

As we tromped up the stairs to my place, Benji gasped. "Oh! I meant to tell you. I went to the clinic and got tested. All clear." He pressed his front against my back and rested his chin on my shoulder as he watched me unlock the door. "So, once you get a chance to go, we should be good."

I swung the door open, slammed it shut as I tossed my keys on the table, and pulled Benji into my arms. "I already went." I kissed him. "All good."

Benji's grin broke through even as he tried to contain it by biting his lip. "So, does that mean…"

"I'm game if you are." My heart thudded at the thought of taking such a big step with him. I'd never had unprotected sex. Never felt close enough to anyone to feel like I wanted that. Maybe we'd end up not liking it, but I definitely wanted to share the experience with Benji. He was the only person in my life I could ever imagine wanting to share that with.

Benji turned and raced to the bedroom as he stripped off his clothes.

I laughed and followed him.

By the time we fell naked on the bed, we were locked in a tangle of lips, tongues, arms, legs, and hard cocks all rubbing and thrusting. I rolled to the side and grabbed the lube but left the condom in the drawer.

Benji shifted to his back, stroked his cock and spread his legs. "This way okay? Want to see you."

"I love watching your face as I fuck you." The gruffly whispered words caught in my throat. I slicked my dick and rubbed a finger against Benji's entrance. "Want your legs spread and wrapped around me while I come in you."

He groaned and thrust his hips up as I teased his hole. "Can't wait to feel you skin to skin. Wanna feel your hot cum in me."

I pushed a pillow under his ass and pressed my cock against his pucker. As Benji's body opened for me, I reveled in the heat of his channel and the neediness of his whimpers. "Fuck, it's good. So damn hot."

Benji wrapped his legs around me and pulled me down so we were chest to chest. "I love you," he whispered before kissing me.

The words, the emotion in my heart, the extreme intimacy of our connection was overwhelming. "I love you," I repeated his words. This was different, this was something even more amazing than before. I slowly thrust in and out of his body, my arms wrapped under his armpits, gripping his shoulders. "Is this okay? You want it harder?"

Benji shook his head, the shimmer of a tear at the corner of his eye. "No, this is perfect, just like this. It's so good, so different. Not just the condom thing, but it's like we're not just fucking now." Benji's eyes never left mine as I pumped slowly into him.

"Not just fucking, never gonna be just fucking again. Love you so damn much." I buried my head against his neck and savored our lovemaking. Our sweat-damp skin, the salty scent of his leaking cock, his breathy moans, the soft slap of our flesh, the heady concoction filled the room and delighted my senses. "Jack yourself," I demanded.

Through the tangle of our bodies, Benji gripped himself and began to pump his cock. "God, Rhys, I'm so close. Wanna come, want your hot cum in me." He shuddered as an orgasm rushed through him.

Benji's ass clenched around my dick and I slammed deep as I erupted. My cock pulsed over and over as I spilled my load. I pulled from his body and jacked myself through the final spurts. The sight of my seed escaping Benji's hole did crazy things to me and I used my throbbing shaft to collect the spunk and press it back in as Benji whimpered and ran a hand through the mess he'd made on his stomach.

"Holy shit, that was hot." Benji traced a sticky finger along my bottom lip and grinned as I licked at his release and pulled him close for a salty kiss.

I pushed the taste of him from my lips to his tongue and shivered at how he trembled under me. "I love you. I know I'm supposed to be learning to accept that things aren't perfect and never will be, but that was quite possibly the most perfect sex I've ever had."

Benji laughed as I pulled from him and rolled him into my arms. "Okay, I'll have to give you that one. That was damn near perfect."

13

BENJI

THE FIVE OF us sat in the living room and played a hilarious game of Cards Against Humanity.

Bode, Sage, Kyson, and I had done our usual brunch and groceries, then Rhys had come over with the card game and we'd been laughing our asses off for nearly two hours.

"You guys want to get pizza for an early dinner?" Kyson asked as he flipped through coupons on the coffee table.

Once pizza was ordered, we lost interest in the game when Bode went to the kitchen to get us all bottles of the new cider he was carrying at the bar.

"Okay, question time." Sage waved a paper around. "I saw these in a magazine at school the other day and ripped them out. Thought they'd be fun. Sort of like that old *Newlywed* game." Sage read question number one. "Who's the better kisser?"

"Me." Bode smirked. "But I'm only good because I'm kissing you."

Sage blushed.

I bit my lip. "I think Rhys is the best kisser and just makes me look good while doing it."

"Oh God." Kyson looked toward the ceiling. "Kill me now."

"Question two. What's your sign and your partner's sign?" Sage giggled quietly when Bode squeezed his thigh. "Easy. I'm a Scorpio and Bode is an Aries."

"Benji's a Taurus, I'm a Libra," Rhys said. "Wait, how are twins different zodiac signs?"

Bode laughed. "I was born on May 13 a couple minutes before midnight, Benji was born on May 14 just a couple minutes past midnight."

"Ah, gotcha." Rhys nodded.

Kyson tapped his phone and began to read. "Sage and Bode, here's what yours says, 'When Aries and Scorpio come together in a love match, it can be the kind of relationship where they both wonder how they ever managed apart. Both Signs love power and they can achieve just about anything—as long as they learn to share the spotlight. Scorpio is very focused; once they set their sights on Aries, Aries is most likely powerless to resist.'"

"Accurate." Bode laughed.

Kyson chuckled and clicked a couple times on his phone screen. "Benji and Rhys, here's yours, 'When Taurus and Libra come together in a love affair, it can be the unification of two halves of a whole. These two Signs are thought of as being karmically linked. They're both looking for security in a relationship and they share a love of art, poetry and culture. This relationship may start slowly as, on the surface, they might have few common interests.

However, once they understand one another they may learn they have much more in common than was first apparent.'"

I shrugged. "Well, the signs have spoken."

"Definitely spot on with the security in a relationship and love of art and culture. How do we feel about poetry?" Rhys leaned in to me.

I lifted a shoulder. "Can't write it, don't mind reading it."

"Okay, Kyson, what about you?" Sage asked.

"Me?" Kyson looked surprised. "I'm a Pisces."

Tapping my chin, I grinned. "Hmmm, when is Bay's birthday?"

"I know it's early July. Maybe July 1?" Bode offered.

I raised my brow. "Go ahead." I nodded at Kyson.

"What?" He acted as if he didn't know.

"Look up your signs." I couldn't even hide how much I was enjoying the moment.

Kyson huffed but humored me. "Only because you're like a damn dog with a bone and I know you won't let up." He tapped his phone. "July 1 is Cancer."

"And what's it say about Pisces and Cancer together?" I batted my lashes.

"Pisces and Cancer, 'A love match between a Cancer and a Pisces is a positive meeting of spirits. Both signs are basically tolerant and sympathetic, and Pisces is easily energized by Cancer's ideas. A Pisces mate can open a Cancer's eyes to the world of creativity and spirituality. In turn, Cancer's practicality can be a guide, leading Pisces to the fruition of their dreamy, utopian ideas. This celestial pairing benefits from an amazingly strong and multifaceted emotional bond.'"

"Ohhh, a positive meeting of spirits. That sounds promising." Rhys teased.

"An amazingly strong and multifaceted bond?" Bode pursed his lips. "Like friendship first? You two may not be *together* at this point, but you sure as hell have a bond. I think it would be a good match."

Sage smiled and spread his arms. "The signs have spoken." He laughed. "Okay, moving on. Number three. Who is most likely to deal with a spider?" Sage batted his lashes.

"No worries, I'll save you, baby." Bode chuckled.

"Benji would likely kill the spider, but only because I'd be clueless that it was even there." Rhys shrugged. "I space out sometimes."

"I'm only killing it if it's somewhere it's not supposed to be." I took Rhys's hand. I adored the fact that Rhys fit in so well with our little group.

"Number four. What are they most likely to end up in jail for?" Sage raised his brows. "Oh, this should be good."

"Okay, let's see." Bode crossed his arms over his chest. "Sage would end up in jail for extreme sass and sarcasm. Can you go to jail for being too smart?"

Sage elbowed him.

"Rhys would go to jail for pointing out imperfections," I teased.

Rhys pretended to gasp. "Then Benji would end up in jail for voyeurism. Always sneaking up on people and watching. He's like a damn cat."

Bode laughed. "Pretty sure he's only watching you."

"Kyson would go to jail for illegal hands. Seriously, the

massages you give should be illegal." Sage groaned. "But I'm glad they aren't. Soooo good."

Bode groused, "Still don't like the thought of his hands all over you."

"You can come to my next one and watch. Maybe join in." Sage waggled his brows.

"Whoa, whoa, whoa," Kyson interjected. "I don't run that type of place." He pointed a finger at Bode and Sage. "You two want to play massage parlor, keep it behind closed doors."

We all laughed.

"What about me?" Bode asked. "What would I go to jail for?"

"Bar fight," we all chorused and erupted in laughter.

When he'd caught his breath, Sage handed the sheet to Kyson. "Read number five."

Kyson cleared his throat. "What are they most likely to go viral for?"

"I've got this one." Bode rubbed his hands together. "Sage is going viral for spouting off random facts about a wisdom of wombats and a pandemonium of parrots. Benji and Rhys are going viral for some sort of naked art. Bay is going viral for some sexy silver fox shit. Kyson will go viral with a sensual massage video. And me? I'm going viral when I unload on Dick Silver's ass someday."

We all laughed.

"Naked art, huh? That gives me ideas." Rhys's eyes widened suggestively.

"Number six. Would they rather spend an evening in with you or out with you?" Kyson read.

"Bode would want to go out, but he'd bring me home

early because he'd know I'd want alone time," Sage answered confidently and Bode nodded his agreement.

"In," Rhys and I chimed in at the same time.

"I'm more of a homebody," Kyson added. "I wouldn't mind going out, but definitely not an all-nighter."

"Hmmm, Bay seems to like to be at home as well." I winked.

"That's because he's got a kid to take care of." Kyson shook his head.

When we finished the game of questions, Sage smacked a kiss against Bode's lips. "I have to study. I'll come down later."

Kyson glanced at his phone. "I told Bay I'd sit with Arlo for a bit."

I pulled a hopeful face.

My cousin rolled his eyes. "I'm feeding the kid, letting him play in the bathtub, building some Legos with him, and putting him to bed. Bay will come home, tell me thank you, and leave. End of story."

I wrinkled my nose. "I need to take over writing that story. Plot twist!"

Goodbyes were said and soon Rhys and I were in the living room alone.

"I think I like having short hours on Sundays." Rhys put an arm around me and pulled me close. "We've got a bit before we need to be at the studio. Nap? Movie? Walk?"

"You know what sounds good?" I sat up and took Rhys's hand.

He waited.

"Macarons."

"Yessss," he hissed. "Let's go get some. We can ask

them if they'd provide treats for the studio from time to time."

"Pick up macarons, walk to the studio, make tea, and lounge around upstairs before we open?" I raised my brow hopefully.

"Perfect." Rhys kissed me. "But I'm prepared for imperfection." He nuzzled his nose against mine and we laughed softly.

We enjoyed the sunshine as we walked to The Macaron Bar. We each picked six cookies ranging from salted caramel to Madagascar vanilla to red velvet to pistachio to dark chocolate. Holding our freshly boxed cookies like kids with special treats, we strolled to the studio.

For the next two hours, we savored our cookies and shared bites of our favorites, sipped strong black tea, and enjoyed the background noise of a movie playing on the old television Rhys had brought to the upstairs apartment. When we boxed three cookies each—to save for later—we stretched out on the couch and cuddled together.

"I'm kinda in love with being in love with you." Rhys kissed my neck. "I'm sure it won't always feel this amazing, surely the high will wear off at some point, but I feel like I'm floating on clouds right now."

I traced my thumb over his bottom lip. "I think we're in that beginning stage. But in a way, we're past that point if you think about it. We were at the casual hookup stage, then we started to hit that crush stage, then we had a bit of a break, so maybe now we're a little further into it." I feathered my lips over his and teased with my tongue. "Either way, I *know* things won't always be sunshine and roses, but I think we're stable enough to handle it. As long as we communicate and keep honesty and respect in the forefront, I think we've got it made."

"Is it weird that I'm thinking long term type things?" Rhys frowned. "I've *never* thought of anything long term with a guy."

"That's because as soon as you found anything you could deem as imperfect, you bailed." I pressed my lips against his and savored his scent and flavor.

Rhys chuckled. "True. But bailing all those other times left me free to find you."

We spent the rest of our down time making out and holding each other.

* * *

After a great four hours greeting customers, discussing art with a few, and making quite a few sales, Rhys and I cleaned up the display floor, turned off the main front lights, and retired to the back studio.

"I have an idea after that game we played." Rhys made the statement as he stripped his shirt over his head. "Get naked."

I chuckled. "While I'm pretty sure I'll like anything that involves being naked with you, what exactly is this idea?" I questioned but shucked off my pants and shirt.

Rhys gathered a tote of paints and brushes before spreading a large white canvas sheet on the floor. "I got these body paints the other day. I want to paint each other then make out and roll around on the sheet to see what type of designs we can make."

I smiled and shivered. "I'm game. Is this going to be for our eyes only? On display? Maybe even for sale?"

Rhys pursed his lips for a moment. "I say this first one is just for us. Depending on what it looks like, maybe we make others. Why?"

"Well, I was going to suggest keeping our underwear on or at least jocks so no, um, *leakage* would get on the sheet if others were going to potentially purchase the piece." I palmed my heavy cock knowing that I wouldn't be able to stop the precum once Rhys started painting me with long strokes of smooth, wet, cool paint. And rolling around on the ground in his arms? Yeah, there was going to be more than paint on the sheet.

"Good idea if we decide to make another one for sale. This one will be just ours. Maybe use it as a wall hanging upstairs?" Rhys shook each bottle of paint before flipping open the caps and pouring the colors into their own cups. "Turn around."

I turned so my back was to Rhys and shuddered as the cool paint touched my skin. He rotated between long, sweeping strokes from my shoulders to my ass and short, brisk strokes as he dabbed paint across my upper back.

"So, this is a learning experience. As such, I'm realizing the error of my plan. I was thinking this would be a long, sexy paint session *then* we'd roll around. But if we take a long time to paint each other, it's going to be dry by the time we get on the sheet. The paint seems to be very quick drying." Rhys sighed.

I turned to face him. "Guess we paint each other quickly, get as colorful and messy as we can and get busy on the sheet." I dipped my hands in two cups and scooped up a handful of blue and a handful of red. With a satisfying *smack*, I slapped both hands against his chest, rubbing my thumbs over his nipples.

Rhys laughed and scooped up blue and yellow.

I quickly found myself pressed against him, my own chest now smeared with red and blue as Rhys smacked his hands on my ass cheeks.

He turned me around. "That's hot. Love seeing my handprints on your ass." He hugged me from behind and continued to smear paint all over me.

We each scooped up more globs of paint and applied it here and there, up and down our bodies, before kneeling on the sheet. Rhys reached for me and pulled me into a tight embrace. As he devoured my mouth, he dropped us gently onto the sheet. We spent the next five minutes writhing, rolling, thrusting, and twisting on the ground as our bodies pressed paint against the canvas. When Rhys gripped my cock, I gasped.

"Don't wanna come on our art." I thrust into his hand. "Upstairs."

We rolled from the sheet like kids rolling out of snow angels. The smeared and smudged colors were breathtaking. Knowing that our love created the bold, vibrant piece made my heart flutter. "That's definitely going on a wall somewhere. It's gorgeous."

"Question is," Rhys wrapped his arms around me from behind and leaned his chin on my shoulder, "do we tell people what made it?"

I thought about it for a moment. "I think it depends on the people. Maybe we don't tell acquaintances, but I think family and friends can know if they ask."

"We'll let it dry and then get it hung." Rhys trailed a paint covered hand down my stomach and took my hard length in his fist. "Speaking of *hung*."

We raced for the stairs.

After a colorful shower, we fell onto the bed. Our warm, damp skin stuck together as I eased my lube-slick cock into his tight hole. Kisses, teasing tongues, stroking fists, thrusting and opening, our bodies became one. I spilled into him, pulsing jet after jet. Pulling from his body, I shifted and took his throbbing shaft between my lips and to the back of my throat. I tongued and sucked, fondled his balls, and pressed my dribbling spunk back into his body with my fingers until he shuddered and groaned his release down my throat.

"What did Kyson say about Taurus and Libra? 'A unification of two halves of a whole?'" Rhys wrapped me in his arms and I snuggled against his chest. "I definitely think we're the perfectly unified two halves of a whole." He kissed the top of my head. "I've never felt more complete than when I'm with you."

14

RHYS

"YOU KNOW how we've been toying with the idea of closing the studio a few days a week or having the guys help with hours until, or if, we decide to get a part time employee?" Benji sidled up to me as I washed a coffee cup in the spare apartment.

"Yeah?" We'd played with the idea of testing out certain days being closed, but hadn't decided which days.

"Well, I've got an idea." He kissed my cheek. "Save me the time of explaining it and just tell me it's a great idea and you're in."

I laughed. "While I'm sure it's a great plan, I'd love to hear it before committing to something."

"You're no fun." Benji pretended to pout. "Fine. So, my thought is to try out our closed day being Monday. Then we have Sage and Bode, maybe even Kyson cover Tuesday and Wednesday."

"Okay, I'm fine with that, but what will *we* be doing at that time?" I wasn't sure where Benji was heading with his plan.

"I think we need a few days of rest and relaxation. What would you think about you and me hitting the road to my family's cabin? There's a lake, a hot tub, a big kitchen, a huge bed, rain spouts in the shower." He turned me in his arms and nuzzled at my neck. "Two nights, two days. We leave Monday, come back Wednesday. Just you and me. What do you say?"

I tried to think of some reason we *shouldn't* take a little road trip, but I came up with nothing. Time away with Benji sounded amazing. "I'm in. But we need to be sure we help Sage, Bode, and Kyson at some point since they're doing us a favor."

"No worries. Our crew supports each other." Benji kissed me. "So, we're good? We can leave Monday?"

"Why not leave Sunday evening after closing time?" I let my hands trail down his back and gripped his ass. "An extra night in the cabin with no worries about anyone hearing us when I'm making you scream? Yes, please."

Benji smiled and bit his lip. "Have I told you how much I love you?" He leaned in, angled his head, and brushed his soft lips over mine before teasing with his tongue.

When I opened for him, Benji's hot, slick tongue danced with mine and I groaned as he rocked his hips into me. We eventually came up for air. "We better stop or the studio will remain closed at least an hour after opening time while I fuck you senseless." I smacked a kiss on his mouth.

"Is that supposed to deter me?" Benji laughed and adjusted himself. "Fine, but I'm already counting the days until we can leave on Sunday."

"Same. Now let's go sell some art and mingle with our guests."

We spent the next couple days creating, displaying, chatting, and selling. I couldn't speak for Benji, but I had a feeling he felt the same as me. *Holy shit, I'm making a living doing what I love with the man I love and people love my art.* Did it get any better than that?

* * *

Sunday evening, we threw our bags into Benji's car and hit the road. The Silver family's cabin was a couple hours south of Indianapolis. We kept each other entertained with songs, laughter, and just enjoying comfortable silences. We stopped on the way for some groceries. Benji had checked with his family to make sure no one planned to use the cabin, and his mom told him that it was ours for as long as we wanted but we'd need to bring our own food because it wasn't well-stocked at the moment.

By the time we arrived at the cabin, it was too dark to do much of anything outside unless we wanted to build a fire. We opted to explore tomorrow and stay in for the night.

We tossed our bags in the master bedroom and Benji showed me around before we unloaded the groceries.

"Tomorrow we can take the kayaks out on the lake and take a hike. Maybe do a picnic?" Benji put milk, juice, beer, cider, and wine in the fridge.

I stacked a couple cans of soup in the pantry. "That sounds great. So, what about tonight?"

Benji tossed ramen noodles my way and I surprised myself by catching the two containers.

"What about hot tub and wine?" Benji asked.

"Perfect." I grabbed an ice bucket from the cabinet and gathered ice from the freezer's maker.

Benji retrieved the wine and slipped it into the ice bucket. "Let's set up the area and start the tub, then we can change."

"By change do you mean get naked? Is there any reason to pretend we need swim trunks? Pretty sure we both know I'm going to be fucking you in that hot tub, no reason to put on new clothes that will just need removed." I ran my hands up Benji's shirt and delighted in the way he shivered.

"Fine, we'll take the wine out, light some candles, turn on the tub and get naked. Better?" Benji chuckled. "Always assuming I want your cock. Maybe I just wanted to cuddle and talk."

I snorted and rubbed my knuckles over the bulge in his pants. "Is that why you're already getting hard? Because you want to cuddle and talk?"

Benji huffed. "Maybe."

"Or maybe you want to straddle me and ride my dick until you're a quivering, whimpering pile of goo," I whispered and nipped at his ear.

Benji moaned. "Yeah, maybe that too. Maybe that sounds like a better plan."

We laughed and headed outside to the screened-in porch.

I placed two wine glasses and the ice bucket on the edge of the hot tub.

Benji uncovered the tub and messed with some dials until the water began to swirl and bubble. He grabbed some towels and placed them on a ledge.

I found a lighter and set to work lighting the six candles placed around the porch. When I turned around, Benji had stripped naked and stood there wearing nothing but a grin.

"Come on, catch up." He stroked his dick as he padded toward me.

My clothes were off and tossed to the side in five seconds. I closed the space between us and pulled him into my arms. Our solid chests met and my nipples tightened as his warm skin and coarse hair rubbed them. Our bodies connected from lips and chins to chests and abdomens to thighs and knees. I loved the way every connection was hard against hard, rough against rough, heat against heat. There was nothing soft or fragile between us and I reveled in the muscles and angles and strength. I'd been with other men, but never had my body fit so perfectly and felt so at home as it did with Benji.

We eventually made our way to the hot tub and climbed in. We sank into the hot water and groaned. The water was amazing. Benji sat on the bench seat and I nestled my back to his front. He rubbed my shoulders and neck.

"God, that feels amazing. Maybe not Kyson level amazing, but definitely good." I leaned my head back on Benji's shoulder and shivered as his hands trailed down my chest to my abs and back to my pecs.

"Yeah, well, Kyson's massages may be top notch, but he's not going to impale himself on your cock and ride you until you come deep in his ass, so I guess you can decide which one of us is better." He teased and pinched my nipples, rolling them between his fingers and thumbs as he kissed my neck. "You want Kyson here right now?"

"Fuck, no," I gritted out between clenched teeth as Benji continued to toy with my sensitive nipples. "I want you to get your sweet ass on my dick." I moved across the tub to a higher ledge seat so I could lean back and was more out of the water.

Benji followed me and straddled my lap.

I fisted both of our cocks in my hand and stroked as we kissed, but soon, Benji pulled away and shifted so my dick was nestled in his crack. He reached behind and directed my hard shaft to his entrance and inched himself down bit by bit until I was fully inside.

I'd never tire of watching my man ride me. The strength in his legs, his cock bobbing between us, his hands pressed against my chest, and his guttural moans each time I thrust deeper than before. Water splashed and sloshed all around us, but I focused only on owning Benji's ass. Too soon, my balls drew up tight and I roared my release into his tight hole.

When Benji's body had milked every drop from my cock, I slowly slid from him.

"You're not done," Benji murmured against my mouth as he kissed me. He pulled me to a different seat, a deep set one that put me level with his cock as he stood in front of me. "Suck me."

I opened greedily and moaned around Benji's shaft as he fucked my face. I loved the pull of his hands in my hair, the brief sensation of choking when his cock touched the back of my throat, and the dirty words Benji growled as he thrust in and out of my mouth before stilling and pouring himself down my throat.

A cool breeze chilled us as we caught our breath and built up enough strength to move from the hot tub. By the time we dried off and made it to the bedroom, I felt as if I could sleep for a week. We curled together under the plush comforter completely sated.

We took turns fucking each other a few times during the night and didn't wake until late morning. Time away with Benji was proving to be something I didn't even realize I needed.

* * *

I'd never been much of a nature guy. Well, that's not completely accurate. I loved the beauty of nature, I just didn't like the bugs and dirt of nature so much. But Benji and I spent about two hours kayaking on the lake the next day, and I was sure I'd never had more fun. The peace and tranquility of the water, the sunshine, and the sounds of nature surrounded us and provided the perfect backdrop for Benji and I to talk about anything and everything.

We enjoyed a picnic lunch in the cabin's backyard and napped for a while cuddled on a blanket spread across the grass before setting out on a hike. As someone who wasn't crazy about being one with nature, I was slightly hesitant to venture into the woods, but the paths were fairly open and no monster bugs attacked. The woods were quiet and peaceful despite the birds and insects serenading us with their songs.

Benji picked up a couple sticks. Handing one to me, he continued walking along the path.

"Am I supposed to beat you with it?" I poked him in the butt with my stick.

He laughed and slowed up before grabbing me in a head lock and ruffling my hair. "No, asshole. It's a hiking stick, a walking stick. Hiking is always better with a stick."

We walked a bit deeper into the woods. When we came to an open area with amazing lighting, we took selfies with trees and plants as our background. Benji insisted on cheesy cheek-kissing shots and I wanted a picture of a real kiss.

The real kiss lingered and turned more heated than I'd planned it to be. Before I knew what he had planned, Benji backed me against a tree and dropped to his knees. With a wicked gleam in his eyes, he stared up at me as he unbuttoned and unzipped my pants. Pulling out my cock, he stroked it and licked my slit.

"Wanna taste you." He swirled his tongue around my head and slid his lips around my length, taking me deep.

The suddenness of his actions had me ready to bust a nut. With the sensation of bark biting into my shoulders and above my waistband where my shirt had ridden up, I fucked Benji's pretty pink lips with a fist in his hair to hold him in place as I thrust deep. "Fuck, I'm gonna come." My words were barely out when I erupted hot and hard in his throat. I shivered as he took every drop and licked me clean.

Benji ran his hands up my body as he stood to kiss me, his tongue thrusting my salty flavor back at me.

"My turn," I growled against his lips.

Benji grinned. He unbuttoned, unzipped, and pulled his hard cock out in seconds before forcing me to my knees. "Spread your legs and straddle the tree so you can be pressed against it."

Uncomfortable in my kneeling position, I spread my

knees and shifted backwards until I was flush with the tree.

"Arms above your head. Wrap them around the tree. No touching."

I obliged.

Benji slapped his shaft against my cheek and then smeared precum along my lips. "Suck it."

Not needing to be told twice, I opened to tongue his slit before sucking him deep. My hands struggled to find purchase on the rough bark. The wood was buried in the flesh of my back as Benji pressed me hard against the tree. My thighs ached, spread wide around the trunk, and I winced as a root knot dug into my knee. The scent and flavor of Benji filled me as his bitter saltiness alighted my tongue and my nose nudged the base of his dick, his neatly trimmed hair tickling as I attempted to breathe without gagging on his fat cock.

"Gonna come and you're gonna take it, swallow every drop, lick my cock clean." Benji continued the punishing pace, his shaft bumping the back of my throat until tears leaked from my eyes, one hand fisted in my hair and pulling hard. "You want my load?" He paused and angled my head to look up.

I nodded, imagining what a picture we made. My lips stretched wide around his cock while he fucked my mouth against a tree, saliva dripping from my chin, his fist gripping my hair. The image was erotic as fuck and I blinked while waiting for Benji to give me what I wanted.

"Swallow me," he demanded and his cock pulsed ribbons of cum on my tongue. I swallowed and immediately wanted more.

Benji pulled from my mouth. "Lick me clean."

I cleaned him thoroughly. With my legs beginning to shake, I shifted in hopes of standing. Benji assisted me to stand and pulled me into a warm, protective embrace.

"That was fucking amazing, sorry if it was too rough or too much," he whispered against my ear and held me tight. "Not sure what came over me, but you were so good."

I trembled and allowed Benji to hold me. "It was good, I liked it." The pain, the submission, the roughness in his actions, everything had turned me on and made me want more.

We held each quietly for several moments, reveling in the closeness and coming back to our senses.

"You want to ride a horse?" Benji asked.

I snorted. "The way you just had me basically reverse cowgirling that tree, I'm not sure my legs can take it." I narrowed my eyes. "And are we talking a real horse or sex?"

Benji kissed me. "While I love the thought of you riding my horse cock," he paused and we both laughed, "I actually meant real horseback riding."

"I've never ridden one." I grimaced. "I'm a little leery of their size."

"Nah, they're huge and powerful, but they won't hurt you if you know what you're doing." Benji picked up our walking sticks and handed one to me before taking my hand and starting back the way we'd come.

"And you know what you're doing?" I was skeptical.

"I do."

"How?"

"I'm not just a handsome artist, I grew up on a sprawling farm with horses. Family still has some.

Tomorrow, we ride." He bumped me with his hip. "But maybe tonight I do my own reverse cowgirl so we have the same sore muscles."

"I'm down."

* * *

Benji's back glistened with sweat as he took my cock, his body opening wide for my invasion. My hands on his hips, thumbs pressing into his round ass cheeks, the muscles of his spread thighs stretched as he straddled me, all of it would forever be burned into my head as one of the sexiest images of all time.

Later, as we cuddled in each other's arms, I whispered gruffly, trying to stamp down the emotions coursing through me, "Thank you for being you, for loving me, for helping me learn to take things in stride." I kissed him, our tongues making love slowly.

"We may not be perfect, but I kinda love being imperfect with you." Benji nuzzled my chest.

* * *

"Okay, so Snickerdoodle is the calmest, most laid back, easiest horse you'll ever ride." Benji walked ahead of me into the horse barn on his family's property. "I'll show you how to saddle her and we'll ride a couple trails."

"My legs are so sore from straddling that damn tree, I'm not sure I can spread them far enough to ride a horse." I was seriously probably walking bow-legged.

"First, face fucking you with your back pressed against that tree was damn hot and definitely on my list of repeats, and you can't deny it was totally worth the pain." Benji slapped my ass. "Second, you might not be as wide as the trunk of that tree, but straddling you *and* taking your dick so hard wasn't exactly comfortable, but you don't see me complaining. It was a good pain."

"It hurt, but it hurt so good," I teased.

"Exactly, now let's saddle up."

Benji showed me how to saddle Snickerdoodle and then had me help saddle his horse, Poncho. He showed me how to mount up, then reversed his movements to dismount and came over to assist me.

"Isn't the saddle going to fall off when I try to pull up on her?"

"Not if it's on right. Now, put your left foot in the stirrup. Push up, lift yourself, and swing your right leg over."

I did as instructed and actually ended up seated on the horse.

"Excellent." Benji swung up on Poncho and sidled next to me. He showed me how to use the reins to direct Snickerdoodle. "She's used to riders and very familiar with the trail, likely won't need much direction." He took the lead and we headed out of the barn. "We won't ride more than an hour. We're both sore already, no reason to add saddle sore to the pain."

Benji acted as tour guide as we traveled the gorgeous property, showing me places where he and Kyson and Bode used to play. A pond, a creek, a barn, an open pasture.

"Wow, I can't imagine so much time outside for one. And I can't imagine what it would be like to have built-in friends to play with. My parents, and then my sister, had me involved in a lot of activities and clubs, but I didn't have a lot of opportunity to play outside. We spent time outside, but it was to walk to a lesson, walk to a club activity, structured play at a park. Not sure if I'd even know how to just play outside without structure." I listened to my words and wondered for the first time if maybe my lack of unstructured play as a child had anything to do with being unable to flow with change, accept when things didn't go as planned, and deal with imperfections when they affected me personally. "You know, I'm thinking that I have a lot of issues," I said after my stretch of thought-filled silence.

"We'll learn and tackle our issues together." Benji winked. He stopped Poncho next to a burbling creek.

Snickerdoodle followed suit. Pretty sure she would have toured me around the property and back to the barn without a single shift of the reins on my part.

Benji climbed off Poncho. "Pit stop, we're going to play for a bit."

I raised my brows, not exactly sure what he meant, but I got off Snickerdoodle and took his hand. "What's up?"

"One of my very favorite things to do as a kid was wade in the creek." Benji slipped off his shoes and peeled off his socks before rolling up his pant legs.

I wrinkled my nose. "But it's muddy, and aren't there like crabs and snakes and worms?"

"Crabs, no. Crawdads, or crawfish, maybe. Snakes, not likely *in* the water. Worms, not in the water. Maybe some minnows. The bottom is muddy, but there are also a lot of rocks to walk on. We'll stay on those for now if you want." He pulled me close and kissed me. "But I promise a little mud won't hurt you."

I removed my shoes and socks. I hated the scratch of grass on my feet. After rolling up my pant legs, I watched Benji.

He waded into the creek. "Damn, that's cold."

"Ringing endorsement. How 'bout I just stay here while you have your fun?"

Benji gestured for me to join him.

I waded in slowly and the icy water took my breath away.

"When you walk on the flat rocks, be careful because they can be slick."

Benji's words were no sooner out of his mouth than I stepped on a slick, flat rock, my foot slipped, and I landed on my ass with cold water up to my waist. "Fuck," I gasped.

Benji was at my side within two seconds. "Shit, are you okay?"

"My ass hurts, I'm cold, and my pride is wounded, but I'm okay." I let Benji pull me to my feet.

"Can you hold your shoes and socks? I'll have you ride on Poncho with me and lead Snickerdoodle." Benji glanced between the two horses. "Since you're so wet, it's better that you don't soak your shoes too."

Within a couple minutes, we were situated on Poncho with Snickerdoodle in tow. "You'll be as wet as me soon," I said as my wet jeans plastered against Benji's thighs.

"Good thing about wet clothes is they dry. We'll be a little uncomfortable, but we'll survive." Benji clicked and maneuvered the reins to direct Poncho back to the barn. "You okay?"

"Yeah, just sore and embarrassed. I hate being wet like this." I was mad at myself for ruining Benji's play time in the creek, but I was also feeling more than prickly at being soaked and cold.

As we rode from the sprawling pasture to the horse barn, Benji tensed. "Fuck," he muttered.

"What's wrong?" My heart fluttered. Benji was my calm, my anchor. If he was upset, I knew something was wrong.

"Porn Brother numero uno. Guess you'll be meeting the infamous Dick Silver." Benji gave a slight gesture toward the barn.

I glanced around him to see a man standing by the fence. He maybe was attractive in his younger years, but he didn't appear to be aging well. How he fathered men as attractive as Bode and Benji was beyond me. Perhaps I was already biased, but I didn't like him and wrinkled my nose. "Can't we just ignore him and leave? I'm wet, cold, and sore. I don't want to talk to your asshole dad." Anxiety kicked in. I hated to sound like a whiney brat, but I didn't want to deal with drama. Turning my back, walking away, hiding was easier.

"We won't stay long. But we have to brush the horses, put away the tack, give them some water and food. He can talk until his little heart is content while we do that, then we're out of here." Benji reached back and squeezed my knee.

The gesture should have brought comfort, but in my uncomfortable, stressed state it just made me feel closed in, itchy, and breathless.

Benji led the horses past Dick and straight into the barn.

By the time we'd reached the ground, Benji's dad had sauntered in and was standing with a smarmy grin.

"Well, howdy," he said in a fake country drawl. "Didn't know you were bringing a *friend* to the property. Thought you were just soiling the cabin."

I immediately bristled and my breathing became uneven. I did *not* want to deal with drama.

"Don't be rude," Benji snapped. "Cabin was great. Wanted to show Rhys the property and take him horseback riding. Heading home in just a bit. Rhys, my dad Dick Silver. Dad, my boyfriend and business partner, Rhys Golden."

I swallowed the lump in my throat. I knew it was rude, but I had no desire to shake the man's hand. "Nice to meet you," I lied through my teeth. "I'd shake, but I'm a bit wet and dirty."

Dick scrunched up his face. "Same. Pretty sure I don't even want to know why you're soaked through." He turned his attention to Benji. "So, you went ahead with that damn studio screw-up? Mark my words, it's a mistake."

"Didn't ask for your opinion. The Silver and Gold Creative is open and doing well. Thanks for asking." Benji removed Snickerdoodle's saddle.

"Should have sued or moved to a better place. Gonna come back and bite you in the ass." Dick waved a hand in the air. "Art studio is a risk in itself. Probably can't sell enough to pay the lease *and* make a living." The man glanced my way. "And when the love connection comes to an end, what then? How's that going to work? Just about as bad at business as your damn brother. Just waiting for when he has to come crawling back with his tail tucked between his legs to admit he failed and needs my money."

"The Silver and Gold Creative is thriving. Our

relationship is none of your business." Benji hefted the second saddle from Poncho. "And Bode is an amazing businessman. The Salty Lizard is doing great. We all are. No thanks to our upbringing." He finished putting away the horse supplies and wiping down the animals. "Now, if you'll excuse us, we need to hit the road."

Dick huffed.

"Pleasure as always, *Dad*." Benji tipped an imaginary hat, took my hand, and led me to the car.

I could barely breathe when we reached the car. My teeth chattered, my heart nearly pounded out of my chest, and I worried I was going to puke.

Without a word, Benji dug in my bag for a change of clothes. "You feel okay? Hurt anywhere?"

"Nah, mostly just my pride at this point. Maybe a little bruised and stiff tomorrow, but I'll live."

Benji nodded and tossed me the clothes. "Change into these dry ones. Throw your wet stuff in the trunk."

Hiding behind the car, I stripped out of my wet pants and underwear and quickly pulled on the dry ones. Once I'd changed my shirt and put my socks and shoes back on, I tossed everything in the trunk and silently got in the vehicle.

About five minutes into the drive, Benji glanced my way. "Sorry about that. You okay? I'm kinda getting the vibe that you're freaking out and I'm not sure how to handle that."

I shook my head. "I just really don't know that I can deal with that type of drama. The rudeness, the hatefulness, the nastiness. I love you, but the thought of that type of interaction every time we're around your family makes me sick." I ran a hand over my face. "How does your mom deal with that?"

Benji was quiet for several beats. "My mom and my aunt are best friends. I'm not saying I think it's right, but I think they stay with Dick and Rod for the financial stability. They love their children, they have money to do whatever they'd like, they volunteer and donate to charities, they have each other. They tolerate their husbands because they're used to a certain lifestyle. I try not to judge." He glanced my way again and took a deep breath. "Only you can decide if you can stay with me knowing that Dick and Rod *are* part of my life. But I'd like to ask that you evaluate what exactly Dick's presence and his behavior affected. It was annoying, but we're grown men and his words can't harm us. I swat him away like a damn mosquito and I choose not to spend much time with him at all. Dick has no bearing on my life. He doesn't change that I love you. He doesn't change that I'm happy with my studio and my relationship and my life. Dick Silver has no control over my life. I see him a couple times a year. I don't let him bait me or talk down to me. I defend Bode and Kyson when it's called for. Beyond that, I enjoy my mom and my aunt, spend time with them as much as I can, and allow my mom to spend Dick's hard-earned money on me when she feels like it." He took my hand and squeezed. "But I can't force you to be with me and part of my family if that's going to be too much for you. While I want nothing more than you to stand by me and deal with the good *and* the bad, I won't force you."

I nodded, pulled my hand from his, and turned to face the window. "I need some time to think." We rode the rest of the way in silence. My heart wanted to tell Benji that his family drama wouldn't be an issue for me, but my head couldn't wrap around the thought of facing that type of crazy, dramatic chaos even if just a couple times a year.

When Benji dropped me off, he walked me to my door. "I'll give you a day or so. I love you and I want to make this work, but the ball's in your court." He kissed me and walked away.

I texted Caroline the moment I walked into my apartment.

An hour later, she was at my door. She shoved a large album-type book into my hands as she breezed past me. "This is something I should have shared with you long ago. I was selfish in keeping it all to myself, but I see now that you need it more than ever."

15

BENJI

"CAN I COME IN?" A disheveled Rhys stood at my door two days later.

Was this it? Had he made up his mind and he was coming to end things with me? I'd missed him like crazy at the studio the last two days and my stomach clenched to think how our working relationship would change if we broke up. Would we go back to the way it had been when we were at each other's throats and disagreeing about everything?

I stepped back and allowed him to walk in. He carried a large book and plopped it on the coffee table when he entered the living room.

"Where's everybody?" Rhys glanced around the apartment.

"Sage is at school, Bode doing inventory, Kyson at the office." I gestured toward the kitchen. "You want coffee, tea, juice, soda?"

Rhys closed the distance between us and pulled me into his arms.

I melted at his touch.

A hug was a good sign? Or was it a goodbye hug?

"Tea would be good. This could be a long conversation." Rhys spoke into my neck as he continued to hug me.

I swallowed thickly, still unsure of what he was here to say.

By the time I brought two steaming mugs of tea into the living room, Rhys was seated on the couch with the book on his lap. I paused, trying to decide where it would be best for me to sit.

Rhys shifted and made room for me next to him and I let loose a breath I didn't realize I'd been holding.

We sipped our tea. Rhys gestured for me to sit closer. He took my hand and caressed my thumb for several seconds before speaking. "If you'll have me, this isn't goodbye. I have a lot to say, but I want you to know that I'm in this. I want *us*."

I squeezed his hand as my heart soared. "I want us too. I love you. I've missed you." I motioned toward the book. "What's that?"

Rhys took a drink. "The night you dropped me off, I texted Caroline. Basically, I said, *I don't know that I can deal with the drama of Benji's family. I'm not used to that type of family dynamic. We may have just broken up.*" He shifted slightly to face me. "She was at my place within an hour thrusting this book into my hands. She said something along the lines of *I've been selfish to keep this to myself all these years, but I realize now how badly you need it.*"

My eyes grew wide. "What's in it?"

Rhys opened the first page and gently ran a hand over the inked writing. "It's pretty much a journal scrapbook my mom kept. It's got concert and movie tickets, pictures, notes, letters, cards, journal entries. She collected stuff in this book from before she and Dad were married up until her death."

"Oh, wow. No wonder it's so huge. So many memories in there." I touched the page where his hand lay.

"Yeah." He took a deep breath. "And not all of them happy. Not all good. Not all perfect." Rhys's face kind of crumpled. "Part of the reason I was away for two days was trying to come to terms with the content of this book and trying to forgive my sister for keeping this from me."

"Why did she?"

"She was an adult when our parents were killed, got thrown into being my guardian, and had lost one of her best friends in my mom. I think this book was a way to stay connected to Mom. But by not sharing it with me, Caroline took something from me. She would always tell me that Mom and Dad's marriage, our family, wasn't perfect, but I didn't believe her. This book was the proof I needed." Rhys traced letters with the tip of his finger. "Caroline has apologized profusely. She feels bad. I love her and I'm not going to hold it against her, but I do wish she had let me be part of this, allowed me to learn about my parents, over the years. Maybe I wouldn't be so messed up now."

"Hey, maybe you weren't ready for this book until now. Things happen that make sense at the time and then later they fit together like puzzle pieces. Be grateful you have the book now." I placed my hand on top of his. "Would you like to share some of it?"

We spent several minutes pouring over concert, theater, and movie tickets. The names of the shows, the prices, the dates, each small piece of paper was a clue to Rhys's mother and a time hop to the past.

Rhys pulled a pile of cards out of a pocket page. "I seriously don't know how she even kept the book closed there toward the end. I guess she would have *had* to get a new one if not for the accident." He showed me birthday cards, anniversary cards, and sympathy cards. He also showed me cards from his dad to his mom in which his dad apologized for grievances ranging from minor to pretty major if the context of the apology was anything to go by. "She's saved a few in here from her to him as well."

We silently read the cards.

"They had their issues, but the love between them is evident." I handed him the last card.

"Yeah, I see that too." He turned a page to where a notepad of paper was tucked. "This is her journal. I won't bore you with it all."

I nudged him. "You share whatever you want to share, don't ever think you're boring me."

"She's got entries in here from before they were engaged, days leading up to the wedding, days after, years after, Caroline's birth, my birth, and everything in between. You know what I realized the theme to all of her entries is?" Rhys sniffed.

I waited.

"There's good and bad, highs and lows, happy and sad. My mom and dad were about as perfectly imperfect as two people could be. I could feel the anger in some of Mom's journals. She was so mad at something Dad had done or said. I gathered from the book, and from Caroline, that they had some doozies of fights. Sounded like they could get pretty dramatic and crazy." Rhys smiled sadly. "I appreciate that I didn't know about any of their issues. Would have probably scared me as a kid. But, in a way, I wish I'd known so I didn't grow up measuring every relationship against an unrealistic ruler."

"I can understand that." I finished my cup of tea and placed it on the coffee table.

"Mom wasn't crazy about her in-laws." He chuckled. "Appears Dad had no love lost between him and her parents either." Rhys was quiet for a moment. "It's weird how a kid's mind can build something, based on fact or not, and it becomes so engrained that it's the gospel truth. I never realized there were fights and hurt feelings between my parents and their parents."

"You were pretty young." I patted his arm.

"There are a lot of mentions in here, along with cards and letters, about siblings and friends. Mom and Dad both seemed to have some great friends who carried them through rough times. My dad's sister was one of his best friends and my mom adored her." Rhys hummed briefly. "I barely remember her. She was older and died not too long after Mom and Dad if I recall correctly. But they both seemed to cherish her and their friends."

"It's such a gift to have family and friends you can count on." My heart hurt to think of not having Bode or Kyson in my life. Even Sage and Bay were growing more and more important to me. And to lose Rhys? I hoped I'd never have to know that hurt.

Rhys sniffed again and wiped at his eyes. "As I was going through all of this, I found a single sheet of paper folded and stuck behind the back-cover flap, almost as if hidden on purpose." He pulled out the small rectangle of paper. "Caroline had never even found it." Rhys unfolded the paper. "It's a letter from my mom to me. She wrote it only a week before she died." His words caught in his throat. "She had no way of knowing she was going to die, but I think in some ways maybe she knew she needed to write this for me. Knew that one day, I'd need it."

"Do you want to read it?" I tucked my arm into his and cuddled close. "Your choice. If it's too personal, I understand."

"Not sure I can read it without getting choked up. Here." Rhys handed me the paper.

Dear Rhys,

One day, you'll read this and I hope you know how loved you are. You weren't a surprise, we just planned on you coming earlier in our lives rather than later. You had other plans. From the day you were born, I've known you were destined to be amazing and do great things.

I've known you marched to the beat of your own drummer from the very first time I held you. You've grown into such a good, smart, creative, and talented kid. I look forward to watching you continue to grow and seeing the greatness in you unfold.

I know I've never been the perfect mom, but I pray you know you're loved and wanted and cherished. As you continue to grow, sometimes right before my eyes it seems, I want you to be safe, happy, and healthy. I wish for you to be loved and give love, find someone who makes you happy. We're all halves just looking for our perfect match to build our whole. Find a person who will stand with you, stand by you, support you, appreciate you for you.

I look forward to your next art show at school. I know I'm biased, but I think you're the most talented one there.

Your dad and I are so proud of you.

Love,

Mom

. . .

Tears ran down my face. I cried harder when Rhys sniffed and sobbed next to me. I gently placed the letter on the open book and gathered him in my arms. "Shhh, it's okay. They loved you so very much. They would be so proud of your accomplishments." I held him while he cried.

Rhys eventually wiped his eyes and sat up.

"I told you this would be a long conversation." He chuckled and wiped at his nose. "This book, Caroline's advice, even your words in the car the other day, all of them have led me to one conclusion."

I held my breath.

"I've found that person to love me and to give my love to. I've found the person who makes me happy, who completes my whole. I know you will stand with me, stand by me, support me, and appreciate me. I know all of this because it's what I'll do for you." Rhys kissed me. "I can take on the family drama and every imperfection as long as you're by my side."

"There's absolutely no place I'd rather be," I whispered against his lips before capturing his mouth in a kiss that spoke of welcome home, promises, love, and a beautiful future.

Everyone seemed to be settling into our work and personal lives. Bode and Sage were so sweet and funny together. Bode was super protective of Sage and his eyes shone with abject admiration of Sage's intelligence. Sage seesawed between staring at Bode with extreme love or frustration; there didn't seem to be much in between. They were definitely in love and spent a vast majority of their free time perfecting their sex skills. Both men glowed and their affection toward each other filled me with warm fuzzies. I loved seeing my brother happy and in love.

I hadn't yet worn down Bay and Kyson, but I was working on it. Kyson was an easier sell and would jump at the chance to take things further with Bay as long as he could be assured he wouldn't mess things up for Bay and Arlo.

Bay, on the other hand, was a stubborn man. But beyond his stubborn streak, I'd slowly come to realize he had a lot of anxiety, both over parenting and just dating in general. He'd shared that he'd been burned in a lot of relationships; I got the feeling one ex may have outed Bay before he was ready. Despite Bay being quite a bit older than Bode, Kyson, and me, he hadn't done a lot of dating recently. His sister had a lot of issues, then she died suddenly and he became an instant father to Arlo. It made sense that he was anxious about starting a relationship with a much younger Kyson. Bay really did have a lot of responsibilities that the rest of us couldn't completely fathom.

But I knew Kyson liked Bay at a deeper level than just attraction. I also knew Kyson was falling hard for Arlo. I wanted Bay to understand what I already knew about my cousin—if ever a time came for Kyson to give his heart away, he would love fully no questions asked. Bay and Arlo needed that type of love; I just needed Bay to see it for himself and let Kyson in.

Rhys and I were madly in love. It was hard to

remember the junk we'd gone through. Had it been the hardest moments of our lives? No. Probably not even close. But our emotions had taken a rollercoaster ride as we went from casual hookups to the beginning of something more to enemies ready to scratch each other's eyes out and then to business partners, lovers, and boyfriends. I wasn't under the impression that things would be perfect, life didn't work that way. But the fact that we'd overcome challenges early on made me think we were better prepared to face obstacles that may await us.

Rhys was contemplating seeing a therapist to work out his issues regarding his parents, his past, and his loss. His creativity was at an all-time high and I adored watching his skills. I wanted to buy over half of the pieces he made, but spending my own money at my studio seemed a bit counterproductive. Rhys promised to make certain pieces just for me. It was just one of the perks to sleeping with the co-owner of an art studio.

The Salty Lizard was in the black and showed no signs of revenue dipping if the historical trends were to be believed. I think every time Bode saw the amazing numbers on the spreadsheets, he did a little happy jig while silently telling Dick to fuck off. Or, knowing Bode, he probably said it out loud. I was so damn proud of my brother for having a dream and reaching for it; not only did he reach for it, he grabbed it by the balls and owned it.

Kyson's massage therapy practice was booked solid with appointments most days. Kyson was looking to bring in another therapist and was already in the process of hiring an assistant who was knowledgeable in holistic healing practices. Word of mouth was Kyson's best advertising at the moment and locals were flocking to get massages and holistic medicines. I'd never once doubted that Kyson would be successful in whatever he set his mind to.

The Silver and Gold Creative was doing great. Actually, it was doing better than I'd anticipated. I'd hoped to eventually get steady customers and sales, but I'd really thought it would take several months. But we had a lot of regulars coming in as often as we were open, and many of them bought large items as well as smaller pieces. The best part was that our most loyal customers were telling their friends and neighbors about the studio. The power of supporting local small businesses was strong and working out tremendously well for us.

And just when I started feeling comfortable and smug that things were going so well, we were hit with some challenges.

The vandalism and burglaries started small and random.

A bit of spray paint here, a busted window there.

But soon, our Mass. Ave. business neighbors and fellow inhabitants began to notice that the crimes were building, taking place more often, and appeared to be focusing on our street specifically. Yes, there were similar crimes taking place all over the downtown area, but the recent rash of transgressions seemed to be happening more in our area, up and down Mass. Ave., and especially in locations where the petty criminals were able to hide behind walls or objects or even just blend into the dark shadows. The crimes weren't specifically hateful in nature, but more than a few instances of graffiti had included racial, religious, and homophobic slurs. For the first time since moving to the city, I began to feel somewhat unsafe and unwelcome.

The local crime watch beefed up their numbers and set out to patrol more often and keep an eye on things more closely.

Unfortunately, the Silvers and company didn't escape the vandalism. Within a week, the bar, the massage practice, and our studio all got hit with broken windows and graffiti. Bay was dealing with the same at his motorcycle shop from the week before.

"I absolutely hate what they're doing." Bode stood with his arms crossed over his chest, frowning in the middle of The Salty Lizard. "The increased patrols are good, but we need to do more."

"I think one of the best things we can do is remove ways for them to hide. Take away any walls or objects obstructing views and add lighting. Lots of lighting. If there are no shadows or crevices for the vandals to hide in, they aren't going to feel as safe spreading their hatred." Sage pushed his glasses up his nose.

"That's a really good idea," Bay interjected. "My shop is on a corner and the side that's dark and somewhat hidden is where they did the most damage." He rubbed his chin. "I've got some thoughts on adding lighting. Should be an easy fix."

Kyson nodded. "They didn't mess with my building on the exposed sides, they did their worst in the dark alley." He looked at Bay and smiled. "Same for me, some lighting and removing some of the dark corners of that alley will go a long way."

"I hate that we have to adjust just to keep our businesses safe, but adding lighting is a pretty easy and inexpensive option." Rhys glanced toward the back of the bar. "Even here, they went for the areas that were likely the darkest and most hidden. We add lights and flush them out, maybe they'll turn their attention elsewhere."

"Better yet, the cops see them and catch them so they aren't vandalizing other local businesses." I slid my phone in my back pocket. "I'm going to go to the studio and assess our outside lighting situation. See if I can come up with something aesthetically pleasing to fix the issue."

"There's my little artist, gotta one up all of us with a fix that's also pretty." Bode teased and nudged me with his elbow.

A few minutes later, Rhys and I stood outside the studio. The area affected by the graffiti was an outside side wall. The building was angled and the wall in question faced an old courtyard. There weren't really any obstructions to hide vandals, but the location was definitely dark.

"So, our options include an easy out of placing some lights and being done with it." I gestured toward the courtyard and wall.

"Or?" Rhys raised a brow.

"Or we turn it into an art project, blast the whole area with light *and* beauty. Make the wall and courtyard a celebratory piece to highlight the studio, our talents, and what makes this street unique and special." I shrugged. I didn't have an actual idea for the project just yet, but I knew with Rhys on my side, we'd create something gorgeous.

"I like the way you think." Rhys nodded. He glanced toward the wall. "What are your thoughts on that huge crack?"

"Seems to be from years of settling and patchwork here and there. You want to get rid of it?" I eyed the fractured wall. I knew the building was physically solid and sound, it passed inspection with flying colors.

Rhys was quiet for a while as he stared at the crack. "You know, a few months ago, I would have insisted on hiring a crew to fix the wall before we tackle a project that's supposed to bring light and beauty because there's no way I would have been able to see past the ugliness and brokenness."

My heart simultaneously clenched and soared. I knew how much Rhys was working to change his outlook on what perfect meant to him. "And now?"

"Now? I'm reminded that imperfections are what make us unique and beautiful. We all have our cracks and fractures and ugliness; instead of trying to hide them, we should celebrate them, highlight them, and use them to bring people together. Use our shared imperfections to make others see beauty in things that maybe wouldn't have been considered beautiful before."

I pulled Rhys into my arms and kissed him soundly in the shadowed and underkept courtyard. "Have I told you lately how much I love you and how proud I am of you?"

"I love you too." Rhys nuzzled my nose. "Proud of me?"

"You've worked so hard to change your outlook. It's not been easy to learn that you didn't have the perfect family, but you're learning to accept imperfections as unique and beautiful instead of pushing them away or hiding them. You're changing and becoming even better than the man I first fell for."

Rhys smiled and kissed me. "I've had a good role model and teacher."

* * *

The evening of our official unveiling came about a month later. The rest of the guys had added their additional lighting and most of the vandalism had died down. Two teens had been caught with spray paint bottles recently and the cops were hoping the kids would rat out their accomplices. The crime watch was still being extra vigilant, but most of the affected businesses had also added lights and removed obstacles. Most of us were feeling like we could breathe a little sigh of relief.

Once Rhys and I had decided to fix our lighting issue with an artistic piece, we'd spent a couple days hashing out ideas before settling on two pieces that would allow us to showcase our talents. The final products were gorgeous and meant a lot to both Rhys and me.

Our friends, family, fellow business owners, and even a couple of local news channels gathered around as dusk turned to dark.

"Thank you all for coming. You had to know that Benji and I couldn't pass up an opportunity to tackle an art project, so our lighting fix took a little longer than normal." Rhys smiled and took my hand. "As you will see, our light display is a large silver and gold flame with several internal lights that not only flood the area with light, but also shine brightly on our wall. Once we turn on the lights, you'll find that our wall showcases several images portrayed in varying shades of silver and gold, outlined in black along with The Silver and Gold Creative logo and a couple inspirational quotes."

When the silver and gold flame was switched on from inside the studio, a collective gasp came from the crowd. I admired the glowing flame and studied the mural Rhys and I had worked so hard to create.

Same but different, different but the same.

Gorgeous sprawling images of items that fit the theme. Nails and screws, a horse and a donkey, a pen and a pencil, a marker and a crayon, a brush and a comb. The entire wall was filled with items such as these. The Silver and Gold Creative logo was prominently placed along the top left edge of the wall. Two quotes that spoke to Rhys and I were in the spotlight. *What we reach for may be different, but what makes us reach is the same. ~Mark Nepo* and *Whatever our souls are made of yours and mine are the same. ~Emily Bronte.*

The project had started as a way to bring light and curb vandalism, but it had turned into so much more. The wall and flame were artistic representations of Rhys and I coming together, imperfections, and how similarities and differences should be celebrated and are beautiful.

Rhys and I took a few moments to answer questions for the reporters as their cameras focused on the art pieces. I had a feeling Bode had called the news channels; I wasn't going to turn down free publicity.

As the crowd mingled, Rhys and I stood quietly to the side and admired our friends, family, and fellow business owners.

"Thank you for teaching me that our same and different is beautiful, and our imperfections are what make us absolutely perfect," Rhys whispered at my ear before kissing my cheek.

"Thank you for being you, for loving me imperfections and all." I squeezed his hand. "I love you."

"I want to spend the rest of my life being your perfect imperfection and loving you." Rhys put his arm around me and pulled me close.

"I think that can be arranged." We spent the rest of the evening visiting with friends and celebrating the beauty of same but different, different but the same.

16

RHYS

BENJI SPENT an entire week pestering both Kyson and Bay.

"So, are you just physically attracted to him?" Benji asked Kyson while we played video games in their apartment.

Kyson groaned. "Do you ever stop?" He elbowed his cousin. "No, it's not *just* physical. I mean, he's hot as hell. You know I've always had a thing for older guys. But I like spending time with him, we get along, we have a connection. He's exactly the type of guy I'd want to date."

"He's not the type to go out partying." Benji took a drink of his soda.

"Am I the type who spends most of my time partying?" Kyson frowned as he continued to control his on-screen character. "I'm a business owner. I spend most of my time with you knuckleheads, working, learning new holistic medicine practices, staying up to date on my massage skills, and helping with the Lizard. If I get to watch Arlo and chat with Bay, I consider myself lucky."

"Have you guys had any actual conversations about the possibility of dating? Even a few dates, just the two of you, see if there's something there?" Benji, like a dog with a bone, just wouldn't give up.

I was honestly wondering when Kyson would have his fill and punch his cousin.

"We've beat around the bush a little, but he always insinuates that he's busy with work and Arlo, and has to be responsible and consider Arlo above everything. Which I get, I really do. But, *if* we were to date, it's not like I'd be trying to take Bay away from his son." Kyson shrugged and spoke so softly I could barely hear him. "I'd just kinda like to be a part of them."

Benji's brows shot up and he gave me a look that said *Do you hear that? It's so sweet, we've **got** to do something to get Bay and Kyson together.*

Well, that's exactly what *I* thought Benji's look said and I was pretty sure I was right. But, even if it wasn't, I felt my heart going *Awww* over Kyson's words and decided then and there to help Benji get Kyson and Bay set up to at least try a few dates.

"You and Kyson should take Arlo to the park one day. Just hang out and let him play." Benji attempted to sound casual as the three of us stood and watched Arlo paint at his studio lesson. He failed miserably. Not Arlo, he did great. *Benji* failed at coming across casual.

"I want to go to the park with Kyson, Daddy." Arlo piped up from his easel, never taking his eyes from his open paint time.

The five-year-old twins who were originally scheduled to attend the lesson had come down with pink eye and had to reschedule, so Arlo was enjoying a private lesson.

Bay crossed his arms over his chest and gave Benji a menacing look, but spoke gently to Arlo. "I'm sure we can see if Kyson would like to go to the park. But we have to remember that he's busy."

"He told me he likes to play with me. He wants to go to the park." The little boy nodded his head as if he was completely sure Kyson would jump at the chance to go to the park with him.

Honestly, even as much as Kyson was interested in Bay, I was pretty sure he'd still jump at the chance to go to the park with Arlo. Kyson was crazy about the little boy.

Arlo dutifully removed his colorful, wet paper and placed it on the drying rack before attaching a new piece of paper with a little help from Benji.

"So maybe the park? Then try some coffee?" Benji continued in his matchmaking, seemingly undeterred by Bay's eye roll. "Sage and Bode, or Rhys and I, or even all four of us could babysit."

"I'm not a baby," Arlo crowed.

"Kid-sit, how's that?" Benji asked.

"He's got ears like a dog, hears everything." Bay smirked.

"Dog ears! Woof-woof!" Arlo giggled while he painted.

"You have anything against a coffee date? We'd watch Arlo, you guys could go out and enjoy some adult conversation." Benji raised his brows.

"Daddy likes coffee. You should drink coffee with Kyson and take me to the park." Arlo made broad sweeps of yellow paint. "That's the sun."

"Come on, even Arlo says you should give it a chance."
Benji, my little matchmaker, waited with a hopeful smile.

Bay watched Arlo paint for several moments as if he
was deep in thought. Finally, he broke from his trance. "I
don't know that I'm ready for anything serious."

"Wouldn't have to be serious," Benji offered.

Bay scoffed. "Based on the connection we have, I can't
imagine it being anything but."

My heart had another one of those *Awww* moments.

"But I'm doing this on my own terms. I won't
compromise my responsibilities to my son. And *I'll* ask
Kyson about the park and coffee. Don't need you passing
him a note for me or anything." Bay gave a little grin.

He looked a combination of excited and nervous.

Benji smiled victoriously. "I think you're making a
great decision. You guys deserve a chance."

* * *

As it turned out, Kyson most definitely *did* want to spend
time with Arlo at the park. Bay had texted Kyson and
asked if he'd want to go to the park with him and Arlo on
Sunday.

I wasn't sure who was more smiley, Benji or Kyson.

The guys had started including me in their Sunday
brunch and grocery shopping and both Kyson and Benji
were floating high on the day Kyson was scheduled for his
park playdate.

"It's just taking a kid to the park, I'm trying not to get
too excited." Kyson seemed unable to wipe the excited
smile from his face.

"Take it slow, but don't be afraid to let him know

you're interested in more." Bode glanced at Kyson over his cup of coffee as we ate our brunch. "I know Bay adores Arlo, but I think the responsibilities that came with his insta-parent status are pretty heavy for him and he doesn't want to weigh you or anyone down with the same expectations. I think he may be worried that dating will lead to you feeling tied down because of the fact that he's tied down."

Kyson nodded. "I get that and I think you're right. I wish I could let him know that I don't consider Arlo a burden. I accept Bay and Arlo as a package deal. Hell, I've never known Bay without his son. If we work out and take things further, get serious, I'd expect to be in a relationship with Bay *and* Arlo." He took a deep breath and shook his head. "And now I'm babbling like an idiot and getting way too far ahead of myself."

Benji squeezed my hand under the table. I knew he was so excited about Kyson and Bay's potential happiness, but I worried he'd be as crushed as Kyson if they didn't work out.

"So? How'd it go?" Benji nearly attacked Kyson when he returned to their apartment Sunday evening.

I'd had no real reason to stay as late as I did, but I couldn't help but want to be there when Kyson shared about his park date with Bay and Arlo.

Kyson was flushed and all smiles. "It was great. Arlo is such a great kid. Plays by himself, plays well with others. Loves his dad, follows directions while still being curious and adventurous and a little stinker at times. He wants a dog and fell in love with every single dog we saw at the park. We played and got ice cream. I'm sure he'll sleep like the dead tonight."

"And?" Benji prodded.

Kyson blushed and bit his lip. "And we were wondering if you guys would mind watching Arlo so we could go out for coffee sometime."

"Yes!" Benji pumped his fist. "I knew it, I knew he was going to ask you."

Sage pulled a knee under him on the couch and sighed. "How did he ask?"

Kyson's cheeks colored to an even darker shade of pink. "Told me that *someone* had been pestering him about us giving things between us a chance and wanted to know if I wanted to grab coffee sometime. It's not like he got down on one knee, just a simple request to go get coffee."

"But if you guys allow yourselves to spend more time together and give yourselves permission for *more* to develop, maybe you can take the next step into making your friendship something a little more." Benji's face was filled with delight and hope.

"Slow down there, bro." Kyson held up a hand. "It's coffee. We'll see what happens from there. May figure out we're better as just friends."

"I gotta tell you, I've seen the way you two look at each other. If that fire and desire lead you guys to bed, I think you'll be burning up the sheets and realizing that you've got a lot more than friendship." Bode pulled Sage to his side.

Kyson huffed. "Good sex doesn't equal a good relationship."

"You're right," I said. "But a lot of good relationships

are built on friendships. You and Bay already know you've got a strong foundation. If the sex and romance add to what you already have, even better. Only you guys will know if *more* is right, but I'm really glad you're giving it a chance."

"I am too." Kyson waved and headed to his room.

Bode, Sage, Benji and I compared our schedules to see if the four of us could come up with multiple dates for babysitting duties. We decided to offer Kyson and Bay an assortment of options so they couldn't use that as an excuse.

I told Bode and Sage goodbye as they scurried off to Bode's room with sultry smiles. Then I gathered Benji in my arms.

"Well, matchmaker, looks like you're getting your wish," I murmured against his mouth before teasing at his lips with my tongue and moaning slightly when he opened for me.

When he pulled away panting, Benji smiled. "I know there's no guarantees. For anyone. Sage and Bode, you and me, none of us *know* we'll work out or stay together. But I'm so glad they are at least taking a chance and giving it a shot."

"Yeah, I think it will be good. Give themselves the chance to test it out. Then they'll know for sure instead of wondering what might have been." I ran my hand up and down Benji's back.

We made out for several moments like sappy teens saying goodbye before I gave him a final kiss. "I love you. I'll see you at the studio tomorrow."

BENJI

I WOKE WRAPPED in warm arms and a cock nudging my ass. Rhys had spent the night so we could prepare for our day of babysitting Arlo. But we had a couple hours before Sage would be bringing the boy to our place.

Rhys trailed his hand down my chest and palmed my already hard dick. "Good morning," he whispered in my ear. "You excited about today?"

I rocked into his touch. "I'm excited to babysit so Bay and Kyson can have a coffee date, but I'm a little preoccupied with something else right now."

"Anything I can help you with?" Rhys pressed his hand against me with more pressure.

"Well, I've got to piss before I do anything else." I gave him an apologetic kiss and rolled from the bed before rushing to the bathroom.

Once I'd relieved myself and managed not to piss all over the wall, I made short work of a quick prep and hurried back to Rhys. I stood in the middle of the room and shucked off my boxers while never taking my eyes from Rhys. When his nostrils flared and he gripped his dick, I took my own shaft in hand and stroked slowly.

"Get over here," Rhys growled.

"What'll I get if I do?" I took a step toward the bed.

"Eventually, I'll give you my cock. But I've got plans to suck you off first." He licked his lips and I couldn't help but shiver.

I moved to the side of the bed and crawled toward him. "Prop yourself on pillows at the headboard."

When Rhys was positioned, I straddled his ankles and slowly shuffled on my knees up his body. I slowed considerably as my balls brushed over his cock, but continued my way up until I reached his chest. I moved Rhys's arms to hold behind my thighs. "Keep your hands there."

Rhys nodded.

I painted my leaking head against his lips. When Rhys's tongue snaked out to taste me, I pressed forward and moaned as his hot mouth took me in. I began a slow rocking rhythm at first, but soon I gripped the headboard and began to fuck Rhys's face with hard, fast thrusts. Never breaking eye contact with him, my heart clenched even as my balls drew up tight. With Rhys's hands encouraging my hips, I pumped into his mouth a couple more times before shooting deep in his throat.

My sensitive cock slid from between Rhys's lips as I shifted from his chest to his hips. I grabbed the small bottle of lube from the bedside table, slicked my hole and his shaft, and directed his rock-hard dick to my waiting ass. "Fuck my ass like I fucked your mouth," I demanded as my body opened and took him fully into my greedy hole.

Rhys grabbed my hips, his fingers gripping tight enough I knew I'd have marks, and I loved it. He pumped his hips hard and fast, his dick sliding in and out as I leaned forward and braced my hands on his chest. There was no way I'd be able to come again so soon, but I reveled in every single second of Rhys invading my body, fucking me, owning me. He gave a final hard thrust and stilled with a groan as his cock pulsed his release deep in my ass.

I whimpered when he pulled from my body, but sighed contentedly when he rolled and pulled me to cuddle against his chest.

"I love you so damn much," he whispered before kissing me softly.

"Mmm, love you too. Also love a thorough morning fucking before getting our day started. May have to look into making wakeups like this happen more often." I snuggled into his chest.

"I could totally get on board with that."

We held each other for several moments as we came down from our sex high.

"Shower?" I asked.

"Yeah, but I'm not sure I can get it up again, so it may just be a regular shower." Rhys chuckled.

"Same. You wore me out." I kissed his chin.

We climbed from the bed. I gathered the dirty sheets and tossed them in a pile on the floor before heading to the bathroom. Damn relationship was going to require me to purchase more sheets because I definitely wasn't going to be able to keep up with washing them if our sex remained as frequent as it had been lately.

* * *

Sage walked in the door with Arlo by his side. "We're home!" Sage sing-songed.

Arlo rushed to Bode and let my brother swing him up into a bear hug. Arlo was comfortable with all of us, but he'd always seemed to gravitate toward Bode, even when Bode was pretty much being an ass to Bay in the beginning.

"Hey, big guy. You gonna hang with us today?" Bode jostled the kid.

"Daddy says I get to play with Kyson *and* you guys." Arlo giggled as Bode tickled his tummy.

"Yep, you sure do." Kyson walked into the room. "What do you want to do first?"

Bode put down Arlo and the little boy scampered to Sage who was carrying three bags.

"This one is clothes, pjs, toothpaste and toothbrush, a sippy cup, and nighttime underwear." Sage held up a large tote bag.

"Nighttime?" Bode mouthed.

"Bay says the sure way to make sure you *need* something is to not pack it, so he packed things we likely won't need. Better safe than sorry." Sage rummaged in the bag. "Also sent some kid soap and shampoo for bath time."

"I brought toys." Arlo tugged on another bag.

"He brought toys," Sage agreed and placed the second bag on the floor.

Arlo dug into the bag. "Blocks, cars, people, stuffies," Arlo muttered as he pulled items from the bag.

"People? Let's see these people." Bode pushed the

coffee table to the side and made room for Arlo to spread out his toys.

Kyson, Bode, and Arlo settled in on the floor to play.

Sage took the third bag to the kitchen and I followed. Rhys ventured toward the play area while I chatted with Sage.

"Bay sent snacks. I told him we'd get pizza, but he sent juice and snacks just in case." Sage pulled the food items out and arranged them on the counter. "He packed like the kid will be here for a week." He chuckled.

"We should probably get some of his favorites to keep here just in case. That way Bay doesn't have to always pack stuff." I picked up a box of whole-grain cookies, a round tin of cheese puffs, and a box of fruit snacks. There were also a couple apples, a banana, grapes, and an orange. I laughed. "Yeah, I think Bay's nerves maybe pushed him into overprepare mode." I took a picture of each item and added them to the grocery list. "Think we should get like baby aspirin or something?"

Sage frowned. "Isn't aspirin dangerous for kids?"

I shrugged. "We'll ask Bay what to keep here."

"No need." Sage chuckled. He went to get the first bag.

When he returned, he held it up. "This is kinda like the diaper bag, but no real diapers. Just the nighttime ones. But Arlo doesn't call them diapers or pull-ups, just nighttime underwear." He dug around until he found whatever he was looking for. "Children's acetaminophen for the win."

"Perfect." I snapped a picture and added the item to the list. Even if Kyson and Bay didn't make a romantic connection, our whole crew was pretty attached to Arlo. It made sense for us to have things for him at our place since we watched him so often.

My chest tightened at how difficult it could end up being if Kyson and Bay didn't work out. We'd all want to stay friends and keep Arlo in our lives, but would it be too difficult for Kyson and Bay? Would they want to stay friends and watch the other date and move on?

I shook off the sad thought. No need to think of problems before the guys had even had a simple coffee date.

A ruckus from the living room had Sage and I heading that way to investigate. My heart went on sweetness overload to find Bode, Kyson, Arlo, *and* Rhys on the floor with a city of blocks, cars racing around with man-made *zoom* noises, and little people figures being made to walk around and talk to each other. It was quite possibly one of the most heartwarming things I'd ever seen. I snapped a picture and texted Bay.

Everyone is settling in and having fun. It's all good.

Bay replied a few minutes later with a smiley face and a heart.

The *boys* played for about thirty more minutes before Arlo lost interest. I swore the three older guys seemed disappointed to put the toys away.

"It's okay." I patted Rhys's arm. "You boys can play with your toys again later."

Rhys smiled. "What?" He shrugged. "It's fun."

"And I love you all the more for it." I kissed him.

* * *

Sage and Bode were sitting in the bathroom while Arlo

played in the bathtub. When I walked by, I couldn't help but laugh. Sage sat on the toilet seat and Bode was on the floor leaning over the edge of the tub with his big arm submerged as he filled up a squirt toy and sprayed Arlo's face.

Kyson had gone to his room to shower and get ready. The excited smile evident on his face.

Rhys and I were going to get pizza soon.

My phone buzzed. *Bay.*

I thumbed the screen and answered. "What's up? Everything is good here."

Bay huffed. "Glad to hear it. What's Arlo doing?"

I chuckled. "Right now, he's taking a bath while Sage watches him and Bode play. I think if Bode could get *in* the tub with him, he would."

Bay laughed. "I'll be sure to give him a hard time about that."

No one had forgotten how grumpy Bode was toward Bay when they first met. It had taken a while for Bode to accept that Bay wasn't going to go after Sage, but he eventually settled down and stopped acting as if he wanted to punch Bay every time he saw the man.

"So, things aren't going as planned," Bay grumbled.

"Problems?"

"Went down south to get a part. Should have known better to make such a long trip with plans made, but I needed to pick up the part for a repair the shop needs to finish." Bay sighed. "I'm feeling guilty as hell leaving Arlo all day and then leaving him longer to take Kyson out."

"But you still want to take Kyson out?"

Bay was silent for a moment. "Yeah, and I think that's where a lot of my guilt is coming from. I'm really looking forward to seeing Kyson, but that makes me feel even worse about dumping my kid with you."

"You didn't *dump* your kid. He's having a blast. *We* volunteered. And you're a better parent when you take time for yourself."

Bay snorted. "You been reading some kinda parenting magazine?"

"I think I saw it on Oprah or something. Seriously, Arlo is great. Pizza is next on the list. Then a movie. He'll be worn out and probably asleep by the time you bring Kyson home. You can drop off your big guy and pick up your little guy."

"I'm really going to be pushing it to get Kyson picked up on time. I should only be about five or ten minutes late *if* traffic stays smooth. If I hit any kind of backup or construction, it's going to be later than that." He grumbled something I couldn't understand. "I'm going to call Kyson and let him know what's going on, but that I'm still coming."

* * *

Bode motioned me into the kitchen while everyone else finished their pizza.

"Wasn't Bay supposed to be here like forty-five minutes ago?" Bode crossed his arms over his chest. "Swear I'll kill him if he stands up Kyson."

I rolled my eyes. "Yeah, he leaves his kid with us and then stands up our cousin? Not the best plan." I glanced back toward the living room where Kyson was definitely on edge. "But I *am* getting a little concerned. Even if he ran into traffic, he should have been here by now."

I gestured for Kyson to join us.

He frowned as he entered the kitchen. "He's late. Like, *really* late. He told me he'd text as he left his place to head this way. But I've heard nothing. Do you think traffic is *that* bad?"

"Have you called him?" Bode asked.

Kyson huffed. "I'm not going to look like some desperate fool calling my missing date to see where he's at."

I whipped out my phone. "I'll call." I pressed Bay's number. It rang and rang until voicemail picked up. "Hey, just checking on you. All is good here. Hope you're not stuck in traffic."

* * *

An hour later, Sage eyed us from his place on the couch next to Arlo. Rhys, Bode, Kyson, and I huddled in the kitchen.

"We have to keep things normal and calm so we don't worry Arlo." Rhys worried his lip. "But Bay is *much* later than he should have been and with no call, I'm seriously worried."

"Same." I leaned against the counter. "We can let Arlo sleep here, no problem, but what do we do about his dad not coming to get him? He's not picked up on the fact that Kyson is still here rather than with his dad, but he's going to notice his dad isn't here sooner or later."

"We could contact Bay's mom, but I'd hate to worry her." Bode frowned.

"I have this really bad feeling something is wrong. Bay was as nervous as I was about the date, but he seemed excited about it. He went to total radio silence and that seems odd since we're watching Arlo." Kyson paced the kitchen. "If the kid wasn't involved, I'd think Bay was just ghosting me, but he'd never do that with Arlo in the middle. I'm worried."

"Have we all called?" Bode asked.

"Multiple times." I nodded and checked my phone once more. "Nothing."

I nearly jumped out of my skin when Kyson's phone buzzed.

He jerked and scowled at the offending phone. "It's a 317 number, but not one I recognize."

"Answer it, could be Bay." I shrugged. Maybe he'd lost his phone and was calling from a different number.

"Hello?" Kyson answered the call. "Yes, this is he."

Kyson's face washed white as a ghost and he faltered in his pacing to lean against the refrigerator. "Okay, yes. I understand. Yes, someone will be there."

Kyson hung up the phone and took a shuddering breath.

I stopped breathing and knew Bode and Rhys had too. Poor Sage was straining his neck from the couch trying to listen without freaking poor Arlo out.

Kyson swallowed and blinked shiny eyes. "That was the hospital. Bay's in the emergency room. They called me because I was the last number he'd called."

The air was sucked out of the room and filled with collective fear and worry.

Bode was the first to snap out of it. "Okay, you okay to drive?"

Kyson nodded. "Yeah, I'm good. I want to be the one that goes."

"We've got Arlo. We'll make it a slumber party. Go to Bay, but keep us updated. If you get to talk to him," Bode paused and cleared his throat, not saying what we were all thinking, *If he's well enough to talk*, "you let him know that Arlo is safe and loved and not to worry about a single thing."

I hugged Kyson close. "Go on. We've got it covered here. But if it's too bad there, call us and someone will come be with you."

Kyson nodded. "They would have told me if he was," he paused and took a deep breath, unable to say what we were all worried about. "Wouldn't they?"

The four of us glanced at each other. We had no answers, only an overwhelming sense of worry and fear that not only might we have lost a good friend, but the little boy sitting in our living room might have lost another parent.

Kyson started, choked on his words, and tried again. "I don't want to disturb him, but tell Arlo I love him. I'm going to sneak out the back door. Give him lots of extra hugs and stories at bedtime okay? I'll let you guys know as soon as I know anything."

He turned and walked out the back door.

I hugged Rhys. "He's *got* to be okay. He's just got to be. That baby in there can't lose his mom *and* his dad. He just got Bay, he can't lose him now."

"I know," Rhys whispered. "Let's go relieve Sage so Bode can tell him what's going on."

Within ten minutes, Sage and Bode joined us on the couch. Sage pulled a sleepy Arlo onto his lap and Bode hit play on Arlo's movie choice of *Frozen*.

I cuddled in to Rhys's side and curled my arm through

Bode's. Bode put his arm around Sage. Sage propped a pillow on Bode's lap and Arlo spread out half on Sage and half on Bode before popping a thumb in his mouth as the movie began. And then we settled in for what would prove to be one of the longest waits of our lives.

* * *

Want more of the guys from Silver in the City? Check out book 3, Silver & Spice releasing February 13, 2020! Grab it HERE!

Find other great books by A.D. Ellis at https://www.amazon.com/A.D.-Ellis/e/B00K0YJ8CW

Discover freebies at https://www.adellisauthor.com

Newsletter sign-up https://www.subscribepage.com/ADEllisNewsMMRomance

NOTES

If you've never been to Indianapolis, you should definitely visit! Here are some of the great places mentioned in this story:

Love Handle- https://www.facebook.com/LoveHandleIndy/

Punch Burger- www.punchburger.com

The Macaron Bar- https://www.macaron-bar.com/indianapolis

ACKNOWLEDGMENTS

It's always so hard to write this part because I'm worried I'll forget someone without meaning to.

Readers- you are the reason I write. As long as you continue reading my stories, I'll continue writing them. Thank you for your support.

Bloggers- your support, reviews, and promotion are very much appreciated. Thank you!

My author buddies- I don't know that I could keep doing this without our brainstorm sessions, laughter, road trips, meals, wine, and friendship as my support.

Thank you to my betas, editors, proofreaders, and ARC readers! Your eyes and input are beyond important to me.

Brett and Gage- as usual, I doubt you even grasp how much your support, input, and friendship mean to me. This author journey has brought many wonderful things into my life, and you both are two of the BEST! I'm blessed to call you friends.

My family and friends- thank you for your love and support, always.

ABOUT THE AUTHOR

A.D. Ellis is an Indiana girl, born and raised. She spends much of her time in central Indiana as an instructional coach/teacher in the inner city of Indianapolis, being a mom to two amazing school-aged children, and wondering how she and her husband of almost two decades have managed to not drive each other insane. A lot of her time is also devoted to phone call avoidance and her hatred of cooking.

She loves chocolate, wine, pizza, and naps along with reading and writing romance. These loves don't leave much time for housework, much to the chagrin of her husband. Who would pick cleaning the house over a nap or a good book? She uses any extra time to increase her fluency in sarcasm.

Find all of Ellis' contemporary romance and male/male romance at www.adellisauthor.com

FREE books-- sign up at bit.ly/ADEllisNews for a FREE male/female romance.

Sign up at http://www.subscribepage.com/ADEllisNewsMMRomance for a FREE male/male romance book.

ALSO BY A.D. ELLIS

Forever Better Together (coming soon to audio!)

His Reluctant Cowboy (also on audio!)

Something About Him (6-book box set)

What Blooms Beneath (also on audio!)

The BJ Boys 3-book box set (soon all three to be on audio!)

Find all of A.D. ELLIS' books on Amazon (most also on KU)
author.to/ADEllisAmazon